HER
DESERT PRINCE

HER
DESERT PRINCE

BY

REBECCA WINTERS

First published in Great Britain 2011
by Mills & Boon, an imprint of Harlequin (UK) Limited.
Large Print edition 2011
Harlequin (UK) Limited, Eton House,
18-24 Paradise Road, Richmond, Surrey TW9 1SR

© Rebecca Winters 2011

ISBN: 978 0 263 22236 4

Harlequin (UK) policy is to use papers that are natural,
renewable and recyclable products and made from
wood grown in sustainable forests. The logging and
manufacturing process conform to the legal environmental
regulations of the country of origin.

Printed and bound in Great Britain
by CPI Antony Rowe, Chippenham, Wiltshire

CHAPTER ONE

Montreux, Switzerland—The third of June

"I CAN'T marry you, Paul. Though I think you're a wonderful man, I'm not in love with you."

"Since your grandmother died, you're too sad to know your own feelings right now."

"But I do know them. A marriage between us wouldn't work."

"So you're really going on that trip?"

"Yes. I want to walk in her footsteps for a time. It's my tribute to her."

"You shouldn't go there alone, Lauren. At least let me come with you to protect you."

"Protect me? From what? No, Paul."

"How long will you be gone?"

"I don't know, but it doesn't matter. This has to be good-bye."

The Nafud Desert—The fifth of June

THEY WANDERED IN THE DESERT *in a solitary way. Thirsty, their souls fainted in them.*

The line from Psalms didn't leave Lauren Viret's mind as she drank from her water bag, surveying the indescribable vastness and loneliness of the northern Arabian desert.

Since they had left the major city of El-Joktor, bone-scorching heat had born down on their little group of twenty penetrating deeper into the desert's heart. Forty actually if you counted the camels. In a movie, the audience would consider them secondary characters. But out here where there were no movie cameras rolling, the humped female dromedary played the star role.

Lauren was less than a granule on this endless burning waste of sand where one could be swallowed alive in an instant. Before she'd set out this morning on her forty-mile journey, her guide, Mustafa, had lectured her that her camel was more valuable than any human.

She'd read enough firsthand accounts of desert

survival to believe it. Besides transportation the camels provided shelter, protection, even water and food in dire circumstances.

While she was deep in thought, Mustafa urged his beast forward to ride alongside her. He talked with excitement as he pointed out the huge, awe-inspiring crescent-shaped dunes in this area of the Nafud Desert. It was true she'd never seen anything like them. No wonder her grandmother had never stopped talking about this place.

But Mustafa had no idea it was something flesh and blood, someone more awesome than these dunes that had captivated Lauren's American grandmother many years ago.

"Malik was bigger than life, Lauren," her grandmother had once told her, "the sheikh over all his people. His word was law. He was as beautiful as a god. I couldn't help myself loving him any more than I could stop breathing."

Lauren couldn't imagine a love like that.

She turned her head to glance at the camel drivers in their head scarves and cloaks, true men of the desert no doubt wondering what had possessed her to come out here alone. Lauren knew she looked out of place, a blonde American woman wearing the Arab male *guthra* and light-weight *kandura* herself, just the way her grandmother Celia Melrose Bancroft had once done.

Everyone at home had marveled over Lauren's resemblance to her grandmother. Odd how certain genetic traits skipped a generation. Lauren's mother had been a stunning brunette, as dark as Lauren was fair. Celia had given her daughter an Arabic name, Lana, meaning tender, which had added to the mystique of Lauren's beautiful mother. Both her mother and father had tragically died in a cable-car accident while skiing six months after Lauren was born, but thankfully Celia had hundreds of photographs which Lauren pored over to keep her father and mother alive in her heart.

"Jolie-laide," Paul had once murmured when he'd first seen a close up of Lana, but Lauren had heard him. In French that meant striking, in an

interesting way without being beautiful. When she'd asked Paul what he'd meant by it he'd said, "I'm afraid you inherited all the *ravissante* genes, *petite*. No offense to your lovely mother."

Lauren had known that Paul had been flirting with her at the time. Of course, he didn't realize that Lauren's part-American, part-Arabic mother had the look of her father, the great Sheikh Malik Ghazi Shafeeq. Lauren had seen a copy of a picture of her grandfather from an old Arab newspaper her grandmother had once shown her. It was still with Celia's treasures.

The sheikh had been dressed in robes and head scarf, making it impossible to see much, except that he had a proud nose and wide mouth, which he'd bequeathed to his daughter. Lauren wondered if her grandfather might still be alive today? Probably not.

Now that Celia had passed away, no one else on earth knew of Lauren's relationship to her Arabic grandfather and they never would. But her curiosity where he was concerned had been one of the main reasons driving her to make this journey into the desert.

Tonight she'd camp out under the stars. Tomorrow the caravan would continue on to the Oasis Al-Shafeeq where she'd spend several weeks and hoped to find out more about the man himself.

On occasion Celia would say, "The one thing I see that reveals the Arab blood in you is your fierce passion for life. Only in that regard have I glimpsed signs of Malik. Mark my words…with the right man, that passion will be unleashed."

Paul, a newspaper journalist from Paris, could never have been that man. Lauren liked Paul, but in her heart she was waiting for the day she experienced the *grande passion* her grandmother had often talked about.

Though Lauren had turned down Paul's marriage proposal, she feared that he hadn't given up hope of marrying her and would be waiting for her upon her return. It was this unflagging trait to his personality that had won him an interview with Celia in the first place.

For several years Paul had been wanting to do a series for his paper on the life of Richard Bancroft, Celia's deceased husband. Though Celia had been a young unwed mother at the time, Richard had married her and become a father figure to a young Lana. He had later become a favorite of Lauren's too, especially after her parents had been killed. Apparently it had never bothered Richard that Celia did not tell him the name of her lover, and Lana's father. It was simply enough that she'd loved Richard.

Richard had been a celebrated adventurer and anthropologist and had led fourteen different expeditions into some of the most inhospitable places on earth. Lauren and her grandmother had often gone along on some of his expeditions, amazed at the new sights they saw on their travels. But for some reason Richard had never traveled to the Arabian desert, and so neither Lauren nor her grandmother had ever ventured there either. Whether it was because her grand-mother considered it too sacred a place to revisit with another man, or whether Richard's interests took him elsewhere, Lauren would never know.

With persistence, Paul had finally won the op-portunity to interview Celia about her life with Richard and their many travels. From the begin-ning he'd made it his business to get to know Lauren, too, who had still lived with her grand-mother in Montreux and was helping to compile Richard's many notes and diaries into a book for publication.

Celia had found Paul charming. Lauren had, too, but for her their relationship had been strictly platonic; her heart wasn't involved. Her grand-mother had known that, but one day had con-fessed to Lauren that her greatest fear was to leave her beloved granddaughter alone without a companion to share her life.

"I won't always be alone," she had assured Celia. "Like you, I plan to travel and do some-thing worthwhile with my life. In time someone will come along." Lauren hadn't wanted to cause her dying grandmother any unnecessary anxiety, but there'd always been honesty between them.

Once Celia was buried, Lauren had made preparations for this trip to the Oasis Al-Shafeeq. She had needed to see the place where her grandmother—romantic to the depths of her being—had experienced a soul-captivating love encountered beneath a full desert moon.

Lauren's hand instinctively went to her throat to touch the small hammered-gold medallion with its inscribed half moon on a gold chain hidden beneath her clothes. It had been her grandmother's greatest treasure, given to her by her lover during a romantic visit to the Garden of the Moon.

She'd mentioned another garden, too, the Garden of Enchantment.

The names had delighted Lauren and she knew she had to see them while she visited there. She considered the medallion a talisman she hoped would one day bring her the same kind of magic that had bonded her grandmother to her beloved sheikh, Malik, body and soul.

With her grandmother now gone, Lauren had wanted to rid herself of her intense sadness and had decided to come on this adventure. She intended to take the same trip her grandmother had taken years before, done in the exact same way.

Celia had been the only mother Lauren had ever known. Now that she was alone, Lauren's whole focus was on traveling to a spot that had resulted in a life-changing experience for Celia. To revisit the spot that had held such treasured memories for her grandmother.

Paul had begged to accompany Lauren on her trip. Earlier in the month he'd met some minor prince from the northern Arabian kingdom at one of the gaming tables at the casino in Montreux. Always looking for something newsworthy, Paul had taken the opportunity to get an interview and had snapped a few pictures of the prince and his retinue for the paper.

During their conversation, the prince, obviously

flattered by Paul's attention and wanting the notoriety, had rhapsodized about the beauty of the Nafud, an area full of great photographic opportunities. He'd boasted that one day he would rule over the entire kingdom. Paul had confided to Lauren that even if it was only wishful thinking on the prince's part, it made a good story.

When he'd passed on this information to Lauren with so much eagerness, she'd hated turning him down, especially after he'd been so good to her grandmother toward the end of her life. But Lauren knew that Paul already had strong feelings for her and she'd refused to lead him on. He was an attractive man who deserved to fall in love with a woman who could love him back. Lauren wasn't that person.

Lost in thought now that she'd had hours to become accustomed to the jostling of her camel's strange gait, she hardly noticed the change in the topography to the southwest. It seemed there was a ridge of brownish mountains appearing as if out of nowhere. She frowned. Yesterday on her flight from Geneva, she'd studied a map of this area, but there'd been no indication of mountains alongside her proposed route to the oasis. She was positive of it.

Suddenly there was shouting. To her ears, the Arabic language always sounded a little like shouting, but these were guttural shouts of a different kind. They sent a thrill of alarm through her body.

"Mustafa?" she called to get his attention before realizing he must have moved further back to talk to the other men. She turned her head to find him. The caravan had stopped. "Mustafa?" she shouted so he'd hear her. "What's happening?"

His camel came up alongside hers. "A sandstorm! We must take cover at once! Pull on the reins so your camel will sit. Quickly!"

Sandstorm. The dreaded violent phenomenon of the desert. At full force more terrifying than a hurricane or a tornado. Only a few days ago she'd read about a caravan many years ago with two thousand people and eighteen hundred camels being overtaken by a storm. Enormous surges and clouds of red sand were raised and rolled forward, burying the whole tribe in its way. Only one Bedouin had survived to write about it.

The surge of wind he'd described in his account now snatched at her cloak without mercy, as if determined to remove it. A strange yellow color stained the blue sky, blotting it out as if it had never existed. It moved fast toward them like a pyroclastic flow from a volcano, but she heard no sound. Panic attacked her because she was finding it difficult to breathe.

Suddenly Mustafa pulled her off her camel with almost superhuman strength and pushed her against the camel's leeward side. "Hold on to the trappings, mademoiselle! Cover your entire head and burrow against the animal."

"But where will you be?" she cried out in fright.

"Next to you, mademoiselle. You mus—" But she wasn't destined to hear the rest. His words were muffled as he pulled the ends of his scarf around his face. One second he was there, the next second she saw…*nothing.*

There was an eerie din in her ears.

"Mustafa!" she screamed, but sand filled her nostrils and throat, gagging her. She covered up, feeling herself start to suffocate. She was drowning in sand. Her head spun like a top, gaining momentum.

We're all going to die, was her last thought before oblivion took over.

Prince Rashad Rayhan Shafeeq, acting sheikh of the northern Arabian kingdom of Al-Shafeeq whilst his father was ill, had only experienced two moments of real jubilation in his life. Both times had been in his early teens. The first was when he'd broken in the stallion his father had given him. The other time had been when his father and the pilot had survived the crash of a small plane and had been missing in the desert for three days.

This afternoon at the mining city of Raz, he

was feeling a different kind of elation mixed with personal satisfaction. This moment had been a long time in coming, three years in fact. Gold had kept the royal family prosperous for centuries and would continue to do so for the next thousand years, but his gamble to do more drilling—a secret those involved had strenuously guarded—had paid off.

Rashad glanced at the heads of the various departments seated around the conference table. He'd called in the most trusted of those who worked for him.

"Gentlemen. Today I met with the chief geologist and engineer who've given me the news I've been waiting for. The recent finds of minerals are so vast, my vision of opening up whole new industries to benefit my father's kingdom has been realized. Besides thousands of new jobs over time, it will mean more education opportunities for the tribe. More hospitals and health care."

Cheers resonated off the walls of the conference room.

This land had belonged to his family for centuries. They had rights to all the minerals and metals being taken from the ground. Various tribes throughout the years had coveted this area rich in resources beyond anyone's dreams and had come against the people of Al-Shafeeq, spilling too much blood, but they'd never prevailed. Thankfully, in these modern times, there wasn't that same kind of strife. Any problems today came from within the circle of Prince Shafeeq's own extended family, but he didn't have time to think about that now.

"Tonight when I return to the palace, I'll inform the king, who will be overjoyed." These days his father suffered from diabetes and had to be more careful in everything he did and ate. "I have no doubts he'll declare a day of celebration. Your hard work has not gone unappreciated and each of you will receive a large bonus for your excellent work *and* your loyalty to the royal family."

With spirits so high, he barely heard someone calling to him. He turned his head. "Your

Highness," the gold-plant manager beckoned to him from the doorway amidst the escalating noise. Rashad saw the concerned look on his face and excused himself to go out in the hall.

"Forgive me for disturbing you, but there was a sandstorm between El-Joktor and Al-Shafeeq, catching a caravan en route unawares."

The bad news tarnished an otherwise red-letter day. "You have eye witnesses?"

"A passing horseman saw what was left of it from a distance and rode here for help. He noticed some camels wandering, but had no idea how many tribesmen survived or are dead and buried beneath the sand."

His gut clenched. "How far away?"

"Twelve miles."

"Assemble a search-and-rescue party to head out on horseback with supplies immediately. Have water loaded on to my helicopter and I'll fly over the site to assess the damage and look for survivors. If needs be, I'll airlift the worst casualties to Al-Shafeeq."

"Yes, Your Highness."

Rashad rejoined the men in the conference room and told them what had happened. The news galvanized everyone into action. They ran out the door behind Rashad to help in the rescue effort.

"Tariq? Come with me!" At a time like this, they would need all the help they could get and Tariq was a trusted colleague at the plant. His help would be invaluable.

At the waiting helicopter where water and other emergency supplies were being loaded, Rashad climbed into the pilot's seat and did a pre-flight check. One of his bodyguards sat in back, followed by Tariq, who finished loading supplies then strapped himself in the co-pilot's seat.

It was always dangerous to approach strangers in the desert, but with the knowledge that his own tribesmen might be involved, Rashad couldn't look the other way. Within seconds he had the rotors whining and they lifted off.

He wished he could fly this machine as fast

as his tribe's famous streamlined falcons flew. When they went into a stoop for their prey, Rashad had clocked them doing 200 mph. Getting to the scene of the tragedy quickly was crucial if it meant lives could be saved.

This part of the desert was known for violent winds that rose up suddenly without warning. Sandstorms weren't so common in the area, but when they did come, they could be devastating.

Before long he spotted cloaked figures and camels clustered together. Tariq handed him the binoculars for a better look. All were waving. The situation might not be as bad as first reported. He gave back the glasses and set the helicopter down a short distance off, willing to take the risk to his own safety.

"Careful, Your Highness," Tariq cautioned. "It could be bandits luring us into the open. Someone may have planned an ambush and is waiting for us to walk into it."

Rashad supposed it was possible, but then a group of men from the caravan came running toward them and Rashad recognized Mustafa Tahar before they bowed down to praise the prince for their deliverance.

"It's all right," Rashad advised his companions. Even as the blades were still rotating, whipping up sand, Tariq began lowering supplies. Rashad shut off the engine and jumped down to help carry water, that vital necessity meaning life or death under these circumstances.

Mustafa, a reputable caravan cameleer from the oasis whom Rashad had known for years, motioned him over to a spot where he saw a body laid out on the sand and covered by blankets.

"This one is still alive, but without a doctor to rehydrate her, she will not live. I tried to give her the little water I had left, but it ran out of her mouth."

"*She?*"

"Yes, Your Highness."

Rashad hunkered down and lifted the blanket off her body, surprised to see a woman lying on her side wearing a man's *kandura*. His fingers felt for a pulse at her slim wrist. It was slow, but it was there. She wore no jewelry on her delicate hands, only a gold watch around her wrist. Rashad noticed that she was already feverish.

His gaze traveled over her, stunned by the sight of hair as diaphanous as gossamer despite the sand particles. Her beauty was a revelation. It caused him to pause for a second before he reached down and picked her up; her slight weight filled his arms, sending an odd sensation through him.

Though his people believed in omens, he was more skeptical and refused to credit what he was feeling as anything more than a response to an attractive female. He hadn't been with one in several weeks. Affairs of state for his father had kept him too busy.

This woman's pallor didn't diminish her fresh-faced, porcelain complexion. A slight fruity fragrance escaped the silkiest hair ever to touch his cheek. Wisps of it, not confined, framed classic features. Her feminine scent tantalized his nostrils and further weakened him in ways his mind refused to acknowledge.

Mustafa followed him to the helicopter where Tariq assisted in strapping her into the seat behind them.

"She was traveling to Al-Shafeeq."

"Alone?" Rashad couldn't imagine why.

"Yes." Mustafa scratched the side of his cheek. "I thought it strange, too. Here is her passport."

Rashad grimaced before putting it inside his pocket. "Is there anyone else who needs immediate treatment?"

"No, Your Highness."

"Good, then I'll fly her to the palace for medical care. Help is coming from Raz with provisions for you. They'll be here soon."

Mustafa nodded his thanks and once more Rashad started up the helicopter, this time heading for Al-Shafeeq. He reached for his satellite phone to call Nazir. His personal assistant at the palace would make certain the doctor for the royal family would be standing by ready to take over.

After a short flight, Rashad put down at the side of the palace. He let Tariq and the bodyguard lower the woman out of the helicopter. The less he had to do with this incredibly appealing female, the better. A team of medical people rushed forward and took her seemingly lifeless form inside.

Assured she'd get the best treatment possible, he told the men to climb back in the helicopter and he'd fly them back to Raz. Rashad still had business to finish up.

During the flight Tariq remained uncharacteristically quiet. Rashad cast him a side glance. "What's on your mind, Tariq? I haven't heard a word out of you."

"It's not natural for a woman to be out here alone. Especially one so young."

"I agree, but this one is foreign, which explains a lot."

"She is very, very beautiful. Some man will

suffer if he learns the sand has claimed her. Let's hope the doctor can save her."

Rashad didn't respond because Tariq's words had sent an invisible wind racing over his skin, lifting the hairs on his bronzed arms and nape. That was the second time within an hour he'd felt a quickening. He didn't like it. He didn't like it at all.

Anxious to get back to work on his new plans, Rashad set them down outside the main plant, only to hear his phone ring as Tariq exited the chopper. Rashad checked the caller ID; it was the doctor back at the palace.

His body tautened. The man was probably phoning to tell Rashad he'd lost his patient. And what if he had? What could that possibly mean to Rashad, except that he would feel sorrow for anyone who'd died in those circumstances? He finally answered the call. "Dr. Tamam?"

"I'm glad you answered right away."

"Did I get the American woman to you too late?"

"No. She's slowly reviving with the IV."

Rashad released his breath, unaware he'd been holding it until he'd heard the news. "She was very fortunate. Is she coherent yet?"

"No, but that's good."

Rashad nodded to himself. "She's going to be in shock while she recovers from her ordeal." He waited for a response, but when it came, the doctor's words surprised Rashad.

"This woman needs complete privacy, away from everyone. Do you have a suggestion, Your Highness?"

This was no normal request from the doctor, and Rashad was immediately alerted. Without having to think about it he said, "The garden suite."

It was on the second floor of the palace with a rooftop view. A private passageway led to it from the main upstairs hallway. Because of its isolation from the rest of the palace, other members of the family had used it as their bridal suite at the beginning of their honeymoons.

No one would be occupying it again until his own wedding night, scheduled in six months. Lines darkened Rashad's face at the thought.

"Good. The nurse and I will transfer her there immediately."

Nothing else was forthcoming, which wasn't like the usually loquacious doctor. An unsettling feeling swept through Rashad. "I'll be with you shortly, Doctor."

"I will be waiting for you." Dr. Tamam clicked off.

The doctor who'd faithfully looked after his family for years had just ended the call before Rashad could ask any more questions. That alone told him the older man was keeping some information that would be for Rashad's ears alone.

Like everyone else on the staff, the doctor kept his ear to the ground for anything that appeared suspicious. One could never be too careful where the safety of Rashad's family was concerned.

Rashad entered the plant office, intending to work on some details needing attention, but he found he couldn't concentrate. With a grunt of dissatisfaction, he decided to fly back to Al-Shafeeq to find out what was going on. After a quick shower and a meal in his own suite, he left for the other wing of the palace in one of his silk lounging robes.

There was a cultivated garden of exotic flowers by the patio of the garden suite. His mother, along with the gardeners, often tended it because she had a special love for them. Rashad had decided on this suite for their patient partly since the American was a rather exotic species herself. He thought of Tariq's comment—*very, very beautiful* didn't begin to cover Rashad's description of the woman.

He opened the doors and nodded to the nurse who told him the doctor was still in with the American. Rashad walked on through the large sitting room to the bedroom. From a distance he saw the patient in bed with an IV drip hanging from the stand placed at the side. He drew closer. The doctor stood at the other side, checking her pulse. When he saw Rashad, he lowered the woman's arm and moved toward him.

"How is she?" Rashad asked in a quiet voice.

"Coming along. I put something in her IV to help her sleep. Tomorrow she should be in better shape to cope with what happened. I'm leaving the nurse to watch over her during the night and give her oxygen if she needs it. I wanted you here because I'd like you to take a look at what I found hanging from the chain around her neck."

Rashad's brows formed a black bar before he moved past the doctor to see what he was talking about. Closer now, he could tell the IV was doing its job. There was more color in the woman's cheeks. Her hair had been washed, and the wavy strands had a sheen like that on the sheerest wings of the butterflies hovering over the flowers in the garden. Her dark lashes and brows provided a contrast that made her even more stunningly beautiful.

The nurse had dressed her in a white cotton shift. A sheet had been pulled up to her shoulders, but he glimpsed a gold chain around her neck. He flashed the doctor a glance. "What am I supposed to be seeing?"

"*This.* I took the liberty of removing it at the clinic before I did anything else."

As he glanced at the shiny object held in the doctor's palm, Rashad drew in a ragged breath. It was a round gold medallion with a half moon inscribed—the symbol of the Shafeeq royal family.

Only when a new male member was born was another one minted. Rashad had been given his when he'd come of age at sixteen. They were all worn around the neck on a chain, but Rashad had broken with tradition and had asked for his to be fashioned into a ring he could use as his personal seal for important documents. He kept it in the desk of his office here at the palace.

For this woman from another continent to be in possession of one, let alone wearing it, simply wasn't possible! Yet the truth lay in front of him, mere inches away.

How had she come by it?

Without hesitation he pocketed the medallion before returning to the woman. With great care he found the little catch to remove the chain, aware of the softness of her creamy skin against his bronzed knuckles; such skin the women of his tribe didn't possess.

Their patient made a little sound, then moved her head to the other side, as if she'd felt the slight caress of his flesh against hers. He held his breath, half hoping she'd wake up so he could look into her eyes and see through to her soul to where she kept her secrets.

The other half of him hoped she'd stay asleep, thus prolonging the moment when she had to be told she'd almost died. There was a penalty for experiencing the terrible beauty of the desert. Sometimes the price was too great, but this foreign woman had been willing to take the risk. Why?

He stared at the medallion, fingering its smoothness until his jaw hardened. An ill wind boded no good. His mother had said it many times. Nothing about the woman or the medallion added up.

Confounded by the situation, he pocketed the chain with the medallion, then turned to the doctor whose shrewd gaze told its own story. There were few secrets between the two of them. "You were right to tell me about this, but say nothing to anyone else."

"My lips are closed tighter than the eye of the needle, Your Highness. My nurse wasn't allowed to undress and bathe the patient until I'd safely removed the medallion."

In the past the doctor had saved Rashad's life on more than one occasion, and Rashad trusted him completely. "I owe you a great deal. Thank you for taking care of her."

The doctor nodded. "I'm going home. Call if you need me. I'll look in on her later."

As soon as he left, Rashad went through the suitcases left by the maids. He did a thorough search of both, looking for a clue that would help explain this mystery, but he turned up nothing.

To his surprise the woman had packed with no frills. Unlike most females, her underwear and nightgowns were modest. Two dresses for evening, one a simple black, the other cream. A pair of high heels, some sandals and a sweater. The rest, practical clothing for the desert. A small kit with few cosmetics or makeup. She packed like a person used to traveling light.

Rashad knew better than to prolong his stay at the woman's bedside. His thoughts would wander down different paths, distracting him from his mission to unmask her. Like the fragrant white moonflower, she held her secret within her petals, only revealing it in full moonlight when no one was watching.

For the good of the family he'd sworn a holy oath to protect, he would wait until daylight to learn how she'd come by the medallion.

Once he'd said goodnight to the nurse, he strode down a long hallway to his own second-floor suite on the other side of the palace and dismissed his staff. He needed to be alone. After pouring himself a cup of hot black coffee, he wandered through to his bedroom. Reaching for the woman's passport, he sat down in a chair to study it.

Lauren Viret. Twenty-six. Few people looked good in a passport photo, but she was one woman who couldn't take a bad picture. Even lying there unconscious, her beauty had reached out to him, stirring him on some deeper level.

Address: Montreux, Switzerland.

Montreux. The town where the Shafeeq family did their banking. When he had stayed there in order to do business, he had sometimes skied at Porte du Soleil, only a half hour from the Swiss town with its exuberant night life. Rashad had no use for casinos or partying. On the other hand, his forty-year-old cousin Faisal, the ambitious son of his father's younger brother Sabeer, frequented the place on a regular basis, mostly for pleasure.

Rashad liked the snow, but he much preferred flying to Montreux in summer. The sight of Lake Geneva from the bedroom balcony of the family apartment mesmerized him. So much blue water to be seen, with steamers and sailboats, when he'd been born in a land with so little of the precious element above ground. Below the Arabian desert there was a vast amount of water, more than the uninformed person knew.

For years he'd been working to find a way to channel more of it to the surface to water flocks and irrigate crops. A fertile land for the growing population of his people. *That* was his next project in the years to come, but for the moment he was keeping his plans a secret from his uncle's family living nearby. There'd been enough jealousy from that sector to last a lifetime.

Rashad took a deep breath before studying the street address listed in the passport. It was in the wealthiest area of the town bordering the lake. Who was paying for Lauren Viret to live among the pieds-a-terre of royals in Montreux?

Where and how had she come by the medallion? There were only eight in existence.

Reaching the limit of his patience, Rashad closed the passport and tossed it on the nearest table, a beauty inlaid with mother of pearl. It was late. He had no answers to this riddle and needed sleep. Tomorrow he'd get to the bottom of it by drawing close to her. It was a task he found himself looking forward to with uncommon anticipation.

CHAPTER TWO

"MADEMOISELLE? Are you awake?"

The same gentle female voice Lauren thought she'd heard during the night broke through soporific waves to reach her consciousness. She felt something being removed from her nostrils.

"Can you hear me, mademoiselle?"

Lauren tried to communicate, but it was difficult because her mouth and throat felt too dry to talk. As she tried to sit up, her head reeled and she realized the back of her hand had something in it. What on earth?

"Lie back and drink," the woman urged. She spoke English, but with an accent. Lauren felt a straw being inserted between her lips and she began sucking on it. Cool water trickled down her throat.

"Heaven," she murmured and continued to drink. Suddenly every nerve ending in her body seemed to come alive, like a drooping plant whose roots took in the moisture that worked its way to the leaves.

Her eyelids fluttered open, but she had trouble focusing because she could see three women with the same dark hair and lab coat standing over her. "Are you a doctor?" she questioned.

"No. I'm Dr. Tamam's nurse. How do you feel?"

Lauren started to shake her head, but that only made her feel worse. "I—I don't know," she stammered.

While the nurse removed the IV from her hand, Lauren tried to get her bearings. The hospital room wasn't like any she'd ever seen before. It was huge with sumptuous green and aqua accoutrements, bringing the apartment of a harem to mind. As her head continued to whirl, she realized she could be dreaming all this and wished she could wake up.

A remembered feeling of suffocation took over.

Panic gripped her. "Help me—I can't breathe—" she cried, unable to stem the tears gushing down her cheeks.

She heard voices in the background. Then just one. A male voice. Deep and resonant. She felt it snake right into her body and travel through her nervous system. A man's hand gripped hers. Solid, masterful.

"Don't be afraid. You're safe now." His accented English spoken in a commanding tone was so reassuring, her anxiety lessened and she slept.

When next she came awake, she discovered the same hand holding hers. This time when she opened her eyes, she saw only one figure seated at her bedside. A powerfully built male, probably mid-thirties. The nurse had disappeared.

A white shirt covered his broad shoulders and well-defined chest. A dusting of black hair showed above the opening. The color of the fabric brought out his beautiful olive skin tone. He had the blackest eyes and hair she'd ever seen at such close range. She noticed he wore it longer than some men, slicked it back from his forehead as though he'd been in a hurry.

His widow's peak suited his aquiline features. There was a magnificence about him. She'd never met a truly gorgeous man before, and he was much more than that. Her heart thundered in her chest as though she'd suddenly been given a drug to bring her to life.

Though he studied her as she imagined an eagle would do before swooping to catch its prey unaware, she glimpsed banked fires in the recesses of those eyes. He was dark and dangerous. Her body gave off a shiver of excitement she couldn't repress. Something was wrong with her to be this aware of a total stranger.

"What am I doing here?"

His eyelids lowered, exposing long black lashes that shielded part of his penetrating gaze from her. "You don't remember what happened to you?" He asked the question in a low, silky tone, almost as if he didn't trust what she'd just asked him.

Growing more nervous under his unrelenting scrutiny, she unconsciously moved her hand to her throat. Suddenly it occurred to her she couldn't feel her grandmother's medallion.

In a frantic gesture, she raised up and moved the pillow to see if it had fallen on to the mattress, but it wasn't there. Neither was the chain.

"Did the nurse remove it?" she cried. By now she was sitting straight up, staring at the man beside her bed.

"Remove what?" he asked in such a calm tone, it got under her skin.

She fought not to let her panic show. Now that the sheet had fallen to her waist, the man's eyes were appraising her. The white shift she wore her was modest enough, but still those black orbs burned like hot coals as he looked at her. But maybe she was being too paranoid because she'd awakened feeling as though she was in a strange dream.

"My medallion is missing. I *have* to find it."

He clasped his bronzed hands beneath a chin so solid, a lesser-blessed male would sell his soul to have been created like this god in earthly form.

A god. That's what her grandmother had called her lover. Lauren had smiled at Celia's description, allowing her that flight of fantasy. But she wasn't laughing now. Maybe Lauren *had* lost her mind. Fear crept over her once more. She closed her eyes and lay back.

"Perhaps if you gave me a description, mademoiselle."

She bit her lip, discovering it was cracked and dry. Just how long had she been in this condition? Her eyes opened again. "It's a gold circle about the size and thickness of an American quarter. Maybe a little thicker."

She didn't dare give the full details. Her relationship to her grandfather was a secret and had to remain one, even down to a piece of jewelry he'd given her grandmother. "Have you ever seen a quarter?" He nodded slowly. "I kept it on a gold chain. It has little monetary value, but it's my most prized possession." More hot tears trickled out of the corners of her eyes.

"Then I'll ask my staff to look for it."

"Thank you." She dashed the moisture from her cheeks with her free hand. "How sick am I?"

His dark gaze flickered. "You've been taken off oxygen and your IV drip. That means you'll be fed juice, in fact, anything you crave, and then you'll be able to get up with help and walk around. By tomorrow you should feel much more recovered."

"But what happened to me?"

He continued to look at her with the strangest expression. She had the impression he was trying to make up his mind what to tell her. The pit in her stomach enlarged, but her natural grit came to the fore. She took a deep breath. "Whatever it is, I can handle it."

"Can you?" He'd asked the question almost seductively. Was he playing with her?

"I'm not a child."

"No. That you are not." A certain nuance in his deep voice sent a little shiver through her.

Don't let him get to you, Lauren. He was a doctor after all and had examined her. Those black eyes had seen everything, so there was nothing he didn't know. "If you won't tell me because you think I'm the fainting kind, I'll ask your nurse. I'm sure she'll oblige me."

"She's gone back to the clinic." The note of satisfaction in his voice set her off.

"I will admit you're doing a good job of frightening me."

He shrugged his shoulders with unconscious elegance. She watched his hands open, as if he were holding a bowl. She noticed inconsequently that those hands were used to hard work, yet his nails and cuticles were immaculate. "A thousand pardons, mademoiselle. My intent has been to save you from remembering too much at once."

She sucked in her breath. "You mean I have amnesia?" More silence. "But that's preposterous!"

The doctor cocked his head. "I'd prefer to call it a temporary lapse of memory. At the moment your mind is protecting you from having to deal with a traumatic experience."

"Traumatic?"

"Very," his voice grated. It seemed to underline the gravity of what he hadn't yet told her. While she contemplated his unsettling response, he got up and reached for a white cloak placed over a satin loveseat. She hadn't realized how tall he was—at least six foot three.

He moved with unconscious male grace. When he approached her again, he let the cape fall loose. "Do you recognize this?"

She tore her eyes from his striking features to look at what he was holding up to her. It was a *kandura*. Lauren had one like it. She'd purchased her desert gear after she'd arrived in El-Joktor, telling the merchant she wanted a man's cloak for herself.

He hadn't wanted to sell it to her because he said it wasn't done in his country. But she had offered him more money than it was worth and he had finally conceded to her wishes and wrapped it up for her.

"Mustafa—"

The camel driver's name came out on a sudden cry of remembrance.

The doctor's eyes flickered. "You see? Your memory is returning. Too fast unfortunately."

A kaleidoscope was filtering through her mind. Bits and pieces started falling together faster than she could keep up. "The mountains were alive. They engulfed everything—Mustafa told me it was a sandstorm. I couldn't see him—I couldn't breathe—what happened to him?"

The doctor's silence puzzled her. She pushed the sheet aside and got out of the bed. Without conscious thought she grabbed his bronzed forearms. "Tell me—did he die because of me?"

His midnight eyes seemed to bore right down into her soul. "No, mademoiselle. Death didn't come for him because it wasn't his appointed hour. In fact, he was the one who saved your life," he said in a gravelly voice. "Without his quick thinking, you would have been buried alive."

She shuddered. "What about the others in the caravan?"

"They survived."

When the words sank in, she let out a relieved cry and slumped against him. "Thank heaven no one perished. It was utterly terrifying."

He murmured something she didn't understand and pulled her into him, absorbing her sobs while he rocked her for as long as she needed. She had no idea how much time passed as they stood locked in each other's arms.

Moments went by before she became aware of his heart pounding, strong and solid against hers. When she'd cried her tears, she eased out of his arms, cognizant of not wanting to leave them. She had to be insane.

"Forgive me for breaking down like that."

"It's the shock of your ordeal, mademoiselle."

"Yes." Reeling from too many emotions, she sank down on the edge of the bed, burying her face in her hands. "If you don't mind, I'd like to be alone."

"As you wish. I'll have a tray sent to you. You need to eat."

"I don't think I could yet."

"It's the duty of the living."

Lauren's head reared back, making her dizzy. But he'd already reached the doors and then he was gone. Not a minute later, a maid came in to help her to the ornate bathroom. After a shower, she dressed in denims and a pale-blue cotton top she'd brought on the trip. The sandstorm hadn't ripped the suitcases from the camels, but it had almost taken her life.

What was it Richard had once told her? *A man who sets out on an expedition has to know he might never come back.* He'd lost men on many of his expeditions, but he'd kept on going. If Richard were still alive he'd say, *You knew the risk, Lauren, and took it.*

In his own way, the doctor had been telling her the same thing.

Lauren could never be that glib about fate, but when the maid returned with a meal of lamb kabobs and fruit salad, she didn't refuse it.

Sometime later the doctor entered the room without her being aware of it. He walked over to the table where she was finishing her food. "Feeling better now, mademoiselle?"

His presence startled her. And thrilled her, too, which was ridiculous. She wiped her mouth with the napkin and looked up at him. He was dressed in a linen sport shirt and trousers. Whatever he wore, he took her breath. Without clothes…he would be spectacular.

"I feel stronger, thank you."

"Stronger is better, but you have a way to go before you're pronounced fit. Your body has been through a tremendous ordeal, physically and emotionally. You must stay here and give yourself time to heal."

He'd brought a tray of food in with him and sat down opposite her. She bit her lip. "Tell me something. Where is *here* exactly?"

"I assumed you knew," he murmured after biting into a fresh peach. "The Oasis of Al-Shafeeq. That was your first destination after you left El-Joktor, was it not?"

Her *only* destination.

"Yes," she whispered, shaken by the knowledge that she'd reached the place once ruled by her grandmother's lover. "How did you know I'd come from El-Joktor?"

He eyed her through veiled lashes. "It's my business to know everything that goes on here. In truth, I'm not Dr. Tamam, but I let you think it for a little while until I was certain you were on the road to a full recovery."

What? But he'd held her hand the whole time. "Then who are you?"

His lips twisted, as if amused by the question. When he did that, he was so attractive, she felt that her heart would fail her. "I'm the head of security here at the palace."

Her eyes widened in disbelief. "No wonder this

room is so exquisite," she whispered. "I couldn't imagine a hotel that could ever look like this."

"The palace is centuries old," he explained. "When I was notified of a caravan overrun by a sandstorm, I flew a helicopter to the scene. Mustafa filled me in and I brought you back here where Dr. Tamam could take care of you."

Head of security for the King?

He not only looked the part, he was the embodiment of her idea of what a king should look like. Bigger than life, the way her grandmother had described King Malik.

She swallowed hard. "So it's you I have to thank for getting me medical help so fast. I—I'm indebted to you," she stammered. It was hard to believe she was actually inside the palace instead of looking at it from the outside like any tourist.

He flashed her a white smile that trapped the air in her lungs. "Grateful enough to let me call you Lauren?"

The way he said her name in his deep voice with that beautiful accent made it sound exotic.

"Of course."

"I saw it printed in your passport, which I have in my possession." His piercing dark eyes traveled over her, missing nothing. "Lauren is a beautiful name, almost as beautiful as its bearer."

Heat spread through her body like wildfire. "What do I call you?" she asked rather breathlessly.

Something flickered in the dark recesses of his eyes as he ate his food. "Rafi. It's easier than the rest of my name which is too long and difficult for a foreigner to pronounce."

Her lips curved into a smile. "I like the shortened version. It reminds me of the spaniel I once had."

"Why is that?"

"Her name was Taffy," she rattled on before realizing he probably thought she was flirting with him. *You* are *flirting with him, Lauren.* Her escape from death had turned her into someone she didn't recognize. She tried to gather her wits, but this was all still like a dream. "Did you ever have a pet growing up?"

"Several, but they may not be the kind you imagine."

"That sounds intriguing."

His eyes glimmered in the candlelight before he asked her another question. "Where were you intending to stay after you arrived here?"

She let out a small cry. "That's right—my reservations—I don't know the name. The documents from the travel agency in Montreux are in my small suitcase. I'm afraid I'm not thinking too clearly yet."

"That's because you've been in a sandstorm and have come out of it with your life irrevocably changed."

Irrevocably. Because of this man, that was the precise word.

"I'll be happy to explain the circumstances to the concierge if you'll give me the information. The staff placed your suitcases in your bedroom. Would you like me to get it for you?"

"No, thank you. I'll do it." She stood up, but she still felt fragile. "Just a moment, please."

Lauren felt his eyes on her back as she walked through to the bedroom and knelt down to open her small case. She found the envelope that held all her travel plans on top and shut the lid, then went back to the other room.

With a wordless exchange he took it from her. Their fingers brushed, sending warmth through her nervous system before he opened the flap to peer inside. When he found what he was looking for, he pulled out his phone and made a call. Except for a few words, she understood no Arabic. The conversation went on for several minutes before he hung up.

He eyed her with an enigmatic gaze. "Is there anyone else you need to inform about what's happened? Anyone to let know where you are?"

"No." With her grandmother gone, she was quite alone.

"Don't tell me there's no man in your life missing you, because I wouldn't believe you."

"There's no one important in my life. Only Paul, a friend, who is probably out on a new, exciting assignment for his French newspaper at the moment."

"Won't Paul want to know you are safe from harm?" His voice had fierce undertones. He talked with so much authority, she found herself opening up to him.

"Actually, I would prefer it if Paul didn't know about what happened to me. You see, he proposed to me before I came here and I turned him down. I'm not in love with him and it would seem wrong of me to ask him to come to my aid now. I think it's best if he moves on with his life and finds a woman who will love him in return."

Rafi stared at her over the rim of his coffee cup. "After meeting you, I daresay I doubt he'll ever get over you."

"That's very flattering, but of course he will."

"I wasn't flattering you." His remark set her body trembling. "What about other friends?"

"They don't expect to hear from me this trip."

"Why not?"

"Because I came to try and get over the worst of my pain after losing my grandmother recently. They know that," she muttered, trying to keep the tremor out of her voice, but not succeeding very well.

"You were close to her?"

There was something about this man that made her want to confide in him. Maybe it was because he'd saved her life by getting her to the doctor in time. Whatever the reason, she didn't feel like holding back.

"Very. Both my parents died when I was six months old. She was the only mother I ever knew. I miss her horribly."

"I can understand your wanting to get away for a while, but why the desert, why here? This part of the Nafud is particularly harsh."

"I suppose it's because it's one place I've never visited, and it holds no past memories for me." *Only Celia's.*

"You're a world traveler?"

"Yes, from the time I was a little girl."

A definite stillness filled the room before he said, "Under the circumstances, I'll leave you alone to grieve. Silence is the medication for sorrow. If you need anything, you have only to pick up the phone by your bed. Nazir, one of my assistants, will take care of you and send for me or the doctor should you need us."

"Thank you." She lowered her head. "I'd be very remiss if I didn't tell you how grateful I am to you for saving my life."

"I only sped up the time so your recovery could take place under Dr. Tamam's care."

"I'm *still* thankful," she insisted. "Be assured, you and your staff will be well paid for your services."

Without giving her a response, he started to leave. Being the head of security, she supposed he had too many calls on his time for her to expect his company like this again but she self-ishly wished he didn't have to leave yet. "Rafi?"

He turned his dark head in her direction. "Is there something else you need?"

There were a lot of things she discovered she needed. "No, but you're obviously on intimate terms with the king. Please let him know how grateful I am for everything. The room is beautiful beyond description."

"It's part of the garden suite."

Lauren sucked in her breath. King Malik had arranged for her grandmother to stay in a private part of the palace with its own garden. Was it possible this suite was the one? The hairs lifted on the back of her neck.

He studied her for a moment. "Are you all right, Lauren?"

"Yes."

"You need a lot more rest before I'm convinced of that. When you're up to it, you're welcome to walk out and enjoy the flowers through that portico. Some are quite exotic. On occasion, the queen herself tends the garden."

She put a hand to her throat. "I don't know why I'm so lucky."

After a slight pause he said, "When word of your near-tragedy reached King Umar, he insisted you remain in this suite as his guest for as long as you want."

His guest…

Lauren's heart beat faster than a hummingbird's wings. Was King Umar a son or a grandson or even a great-nephew of King Malik? Lauren was closer to getting information about her grandfather than she knew.

"That's incredibly kind and generous of him."

His black eyes gleamed. "It's my hope that while you are recovering, the garden's beauty will lift the sadness over your grandmother's passing from your heart."

Deeply touched by his words, she whispered her thanks. Bereft after he'd gone, Lauren couldn't move any further than the nearest couch because a new weakness had attacked her, brought on by his nearness and the potent male reality of him.

She sank down and rested against one of the satin cushions. Her thoughts darted back to her grandmother who'd been a world traveler from an early age. Celia had come to Al-Shafeeq because it had been reported by a family friend highly placed in the government that this desert oasis blossomed like a rose. It had sounded so romantic to her, she'd deemed it a place she had to see.

While wandering through its palatial gardens, her waist-length blond hair had happened to catch the eye of King Malik. What had happened after that had been like a tale from the Arabian Nights tale and Celia had become enslaved by a love so powerful that Lauren's mother, Lana, had been the ultimate result.

Lauren thought about the flowers on the patio, but she was too tired to walk out there yet. Inwardly she had the presentiment that if she went out to look at them, history might repeat itself. Lauren could well imagine being so enamored of Rafi, she would never want to leave Al-Shafeeq.

His powerful image swam before her eyes until they closed and she knew no more.

Rashad stood outside the suite and rang Dr. Tamam to give him the latest update. "Our patient was well enough to shower and eat a solid meal today."

"That's good. What did you find out about the medallion?"

He pursed his lips. "Nothing yet."

"Ah?" The surprise in the older man's voice was as unmistakable as it was understandable. "Then you must have felt she still wasn't recovered enough to withstand an interrogation."

The doctor was reading Rashad's mind. Lauren had paled a little before he'd left her suite. That part was genuine. In fact everything she'd said, every reaction, had seemed genuine to him, especially her relief that Mustafa hadn't died.

He could still feel the imprint of her lovely body molded to his while word of the near-tragedy had sunk in. She'd shed convincing tears of relief.

As for her pain over her deceased grandmother, there were degrees. Upon wakening, her first thought had been for the medallion she'd lost. Rashad had noticed she'd been careful *not* to give him a full description of the gold circle.

His instincts were never wrong. She was holding a secret.

The first thing Rashad needed to do was to ascertain if the medallion was real or a fake. Quite apart from her role in all of this, he wanted the answer for himself. Of the eight male members of the family alive today, including himself, none had reported their medallions lost or stolen. It had to be a fake—some kind of joke, perhaps—but he wouldn't be able to get to the bottom of it until he'd talked to their gold expert.

In the next breath he phoned his mechanic. After being assured his helicopter had been serviced and was ready for flight, he slipped along a passage and across a private courtyard to the place where it was waiting.

Accompanied by his bodyguard, he flew to

Raz. Once they'd set down, he hurried into the plant to consult the goldsmith who'd fashioned Rashad's ring. The old man was getting on in years.

"Come in, Rashad. Your face looks like thunder. Yesterday everyone was rejoicing!"

Grimacing, he sat down at the work table across from him. "That was yesterday." He pulled the medallion and chain out of his pocket and placed it in front of him.

Hasan stared at him in puzzlement. "Whose medallion is this?"

"That's what I need to know."

"You mean someone in the royal family has lost theirs?"

"Maybe. I found it…accidentally. Could it be a fake?"

"Why don't you go do something else for a little while, then come back and I'll have answers for you."

Rashad spent the next hour discussing plans with the engineers drafting designs for the new processing plant. Being an engineer himself, he gave his input before returning to Hasan's lab. The goldsmith gave him a speculative look.

"The medallion is twenty-four-carat gold, but the minting technique with respect to the dyes and style indicates it was made somewhere between 1890 and 1930, give or take fifteen years. I couldn't duplicate what was produced back then." He shook his head. "I have to believe this is not a fake, nor is the chain."

"So," Rashad murmured, "unless someone lost their medallion during that time period, the only other explanation I can come up with is that the family goldsmith at the time could have made an extra one in case of loss."

"But that practice has always been forbidden," Hasan reminded him.

"That's true." Hasan's word was as good as the gold he'd been working with for the last forty years. Rashad's mind shot back in time, making a mental list of every royal male child born within that time period who was now dead. No word of a lost medallion had ever reached his ears.

Rashad knew that no member of the family could ever willingly part with his medallion, and they took them to their graves. Rashad's thoughts ran full circle and led him to the conclusion that the medallion must have been stolen off a dead body at the time of burial. Only family members could be in attendance at this sacred time, so that meant a member of the family had been holding on to it all this time….

For what purpose? And why had it suddenly surfaced around the throat of the stunning blonde American? Had she come specifically to attract Rashad's attention and infiltrate his inner sanctum? Certainly she'd done that!

Such an elaborate scheme for her to glean information could only have been perpetrated by his uncle's family, desperate to discover any information they could, which they could then use against Rashad's own family. Amazingly it had backfired because of catastrophic circumstances beyond anyone's control.

She'd been blown off course all right. Yet in a miraculous way she'd succeeded in penetrating his fortress in a way no enemy had ever done. Someone had coached her well, otherwise why had she held back in her description of the medallion?

Not only hadn't he learned her secret yet, it was possible she'd been equipped with a picture of Rashad from the beginning and had recognized him all along. If *that* were true, then the woman sent to spy on him was the cleverest actress alive to pretend she believed he was the head of security.

Rashad didn't like what he was thinking. Because of his strong attraction to her, it twisted his gut. He threw back his head in frustration. "You've done me an invaluable service, Hasan. I won't forget."

"It's always a pleasure to serve you, Your Highness."

With his business done, Rashad flew back to the palace. After he arrived, he heard from a trusted informant who'd done some digging for him. "What have you learned?"

"She flew into El-Joktor day before yesterday."

The entry visa stamped in her passport had verified as much. She'd only had a one-day trek into the desert. Mustafa assured him they'd met no other caravans en route, no other contacts.

"Upon arrival in El-Joktor, she stayed at the Casbah alone."

The Casbah? When there were modern hotels with amenities, why did she choose a two-star hotel in a poorer quarter of the city, once fashionable but no longer popular for close to many decades?

"Her papers are in order. She has no known occupation, but has been living in the apartment at the Montreux address belonging to an American named Celia Melrose Bancroft, seventy-five, recently deceased."

Had Lauren Viret lied about being the woman's

granddaughter? Perhaps she'd been a very well-paid companion. After the woman died, had she gone looking for another kind of benefactor, this time a male? Or had a certain male found *her*? Was it possible?

"Do you wish me to probe deeper, Your Highness?"

"Not yet. You've done well."

What had Rashad's father taught him repeatedly from childhood? If the camel once gets his nose in the tent, his body will follow. With the help of the elements, Mademoiselle Viret had virtually been swept inside his tent and delivered into his hands.

Dinner with her first, away from all eyes. He needed to learn all there was to know about her. Despite everything he knew or suspected, *he needed to be alone with her.*

CHAPTER THREE

AFTER arranging for a meal on the patio next to the flower garden, Rashad showered and dressed in another shirt and trousers. As he was on his way to the other wing of the palace, Nazir rang him. "Your Highness? The American has just asked me for an outside line from the palace. Should I allow it?"

"Yes." The palace's control center used a satellite tracking device. Later Rashad would check on the numbers she phoned. He bounded up the stairs and kept walking along the passageway until he reached the connecting hall to the garden suite. After knocking, he let himself in and discovered her seated at the desk in the sitting room. She spoke on the phone in French as impeccable as his own.

The minute she saw him approach, she ended her conversation and put down the receiver. "Good evening, Rafi." There was a huskiness in her voice, letting him know she was pleased to see him, even if she hadn't wanted him to know the nature of her business on the phone.

He was shaken to realize that even though elaborate preparations had been made long before she'd set out for Al-Shafeeq on a special mission, the connection between them was real...and rare.

"I'm glad to see you looking more rested."

She nodded her blond head. "I took a nap after you left."

Rashad thought she looked good enough to eat. She was still dressed in the clothes she'd worn earlier. "Are you hungry?"

"Yes."

If it was a lie, he didn't care because he sensed she wanted to spend the evening with him. During the short flight back from Raz, the thought of being with her tonight was all that had consumed him. This kind of instant attraction was different from anything he'd ever known in his life, taking him completely unaware.

"I arranged for us to eat dinner together. How do you feel about that?"

She made a betraying motion with her hands. "If you're free, I—I'd love it." The words fell from her lips with satisfying speed…unrehearsed, unguarded.

"It's waiting out on the patio."

Her beguiling features lit up in pleasure. "I haven't seen the flowers yet." As she got up from the desk, the action drew his attention to her softly rounded figure. He didn't like it that whether she was dressed in a hospital shift or western clothes, the heavenly mold of her body made it impossible for him to look elsewhere.

"Does this mean you're off duty?" Her breathing sounded a trifle shallow, alerting him to the fact that she wasn't in control of herself, either.

"More or less."

"In other words, you're like Dr. Tamam, always available if needed?"

He smiled. "That's one way of putting it."

"He came by a little while ago to check on me."

"What's the verdict?"

"I'm to relax for one more day to gain back my strength. Then I can return to being a tourist again."

"He's an excellent doctor. You won't be sorry for following his advice."

"I plan to." After a pause she said, "Are you hungry too?"

"Ravenous, as a matter of fact." All the senses of his body had come alive around her. He didn't know himself anymore.

"Does that mean you've been out saving more poor souls caught in another sandstorm?" she teased.

Her charisma charmed him to the core of his being and was so at odds with the secret she was keeping, it succeeded in tying him in knots.

"They don't happen that often, but I can tell you this much—in the last hundred years, you have the distinction of being the first foreign woman who lived through one."

He felt her shiver. "I've been blessed, thanks to you and Mustafa."

Rashad took an extra breath. "He was the one who pulled you off your camel in time."

"Yes." She turned away from him. "I need to thank him in person. That's why I was on the phone just now. I called the travel agency in Montreux and asked them to contact him for me."

"I would imagine he's out with another caravan. When your caravan takes you back to El-Joktor, you can thank him then. Now if you'll come with me, the patio is through this alcove."

He cupped her elbow. Their bodies brushed against each other, bringing certain longings alive. He ushered her out to the roof with its crenelated walls. Evening had fallen. The patio torches had been lit.

An awe-filled sigh escaped her lips as she looked out over the desert. He understood it. From this vantage point, one could see the oasis with its many lighted torches, and the sand beyond the boundary stretching in every direction. The perfumed air of the night breeze was cooling down even as they stood there. Stars had started to come out overhead. This was his favorite spot of the palace.

"I've never seen a sight like this in my life."

"Neither have I," Rashad whispered, studying her alluring profile. If he moved an inch closer to her enticing warmth, he would have to touch her. He wouldn't be able to help himself.

"It's magical and makes me want to cry."

She was so in tune with his emotions, he admitted, "Sometimes when my work closes in on me, I get the urge to slip away from my office and come out here to feel the night."

"You *can* feel it," she cried in wonder and turned to him. The glow from the nearest torch reached her eyes. When he looked into them, he was staggered by their bewitching color. They were a rare shade of green so light and iridescent, they dazzled him more than the large shimmering star rising beyond her shoulder.

How could eyes that soulful belong to a woman who'd come here to do him and his family harm? "Are you cold?" He wanted a reason to wrap his arms around her again.

"Not yet," she answered in a shaken voice.

"Then let's eat."

Rashad had instructed his staff to arrange a table for two near the lattice-covered garden so that he and Lauren could enjoy its fragrance. Flames from the candles flickered, throwing the shapes of the flowers into larger-than-life replicas against the thick palace walls.

He pulled out a chair for her. She sat down quickly, but not before his hands shaped her shoulders after helping her. By now her long dark lashes—unusual on someone so fair—half hid her gaze focused on the flowers. "How beautiful," she whispered.

"The royal family calls it the Garden of Enchantment."

Rashad heard her soft intake of breath before she said, "I can understand why. I feel only a sense of peace sitting here. It's exquisite."

"I agree it's perfection."

Goosebumps broke out on Lauren's arms. This was the garden her grandmother had talked about!

Lauren had come to the desert to walk in Celia's steps. Who would have dreamed she'd do it *literally*.

She'd always thought herself a down-to-earth, sensible person, but a force outside her sphere of understanding was at work here and it stemmed from the man seated across from her.

Feeling the full intensity of his eyes on *her* rather than garden, she was afraid to look at him directly. He was too powerfully striking. His unconscious arrogance of demeanor, his fierce male beauty, didn't need the embellishment of this glorious night to cause the blood to pound in her ears.

Something had to be seriously wrong with her to be sitting here mesmerized by this masculine force of nature whose roots had sprung from an unforgiving desert. Refusing to let him know how much his comments and nearness disturbed her, she looked down at the food placed in front of her.

There were slices of melon, fruit ice and tender portions of lamb with potatoes. She'd been so enthralled by him, she hadn't even noticed they'd been served, yet he was already eating with pleasure.

She sipped her hot sweet coffee first. "You keep late hours, Rafi. Have you no wife who's expecting you?"

"A pot needs the right cover. I've not found mine yet."

His admission made her heart leap. "In other words, you're telling me in your unique way to mind my own business." But Lauren laughed as she said it. Considering the looks of the gorgeous if not enigmatic male seated across from her, no Arabic analogy could have been more absurd.

"I'm pleased to see I've been able to bring a smile to your lips. You must do it more often."

"I couldn't help it. Your comment about a pot brought to mind the story of Ali Baba. All those poor thieves boiling in hot oil inside the covered pots. Such a cunning servant girl," she said, enjoying each delicious morsel of food.

His sudden white smile in that burnished face robbed her of breath. "She was that," he murmured before breaking into laughter, the rich male kind she felt to her toes, deep and uninhibited.

She sent him an oblique glance. "I have a hard time believing you're a confirmed bachelor."

"I'm not," he stated matter-of-factly, "but when that day comes, it won't be the kind of marriage you imagine." He drank some coffee while he ate nuts and raisins from the bowls. "It's not written in my stars."

Lauren wiped the corner of her mouth. "If I

didn't know myself better, I'd have made a wrong decision and be in a bad marriage by now. Surely you're in control of your own destiny."

"So far," he said on a cryptic note.

"Do you have family here at the oasis?"

He eyed her for a long moment. "I have parents and siblings."

"You're very fortunate. Have you lived at the oasis all your life?" She found herself wanting to know any detail he would share.

"Apart from schooling in England and France, this has been my home. Has Switzerland always been yours?"

"Yes, but we sometimes stayed in New York where Celia was born."

"Tell me about your grandmother. Had she been ill a long time before she died?"

He'd skillfully guided their conversation away from himself. "No. Celia came down with bronchitis and it turned into pneumonia. Most people in their seventies recover, but she didn't. Because she was such an intrepid adventurer, I assumed she'd live well into her nineties."

"In other words, you weren't prepared for her death."

Tears stung her eyes. "I don't think you ever are, even if you sit at someone's bedside for months or years. She was taken from me too soon."

"Every sun has to set," his deep voice raked across her skin, startling her out of her thoughts. "Your grandmother's sun set sooner than you would have liked. If you made each other happy, then there should be no guilt."

He'd picked up on her guilt with astonishing accuracy, but it had nothing to do with Celia, and everything to do with her inexplicable attraction to him. It frightened her a little. "You're mistaken if you think I have regrets."

He studied her as if he could see into her soul. "Then why do you look, shall we say…fragmented when you talk about her?"

Maybe he'd been a psychologist before going

into security work. She drew in an extra breath. "That's exactly how I feel, no doubt due to her unexpected death and my close brush with it."

"No doubt," Rafi muttered, but he didn't sound convinced. On maddening cue he said, "But I'm glad to see you have an appetite. Even if you're in mourning, it's an excellent sign that you're returning to normal."

Since meeting Rafi, Lauren no longer knew what normal was. She sensed he was getting ready to say goodnight, but she didn't want the evening to end. While she was contemplating a way to detain him, he said, "Much as I would like to stare into your jewel eyes for the rest of the night, it's growing colder out here. Let's go in and enjoy a game of cards. Otherwise I'll have to explain to Dr. Tamam why his patient has suffered a relapse at my hands."

She could still feel those hands on her shoulders. Whenever he made a personal comment, she felt the blood surge to her cheeks. This time when they walked back inside, their bodies brushed. She felt like a firecracker ready to go off.

"I'll warn you now I only know how to play canasta."

One dark brow lifted. "They play that at the casino in Montreux?"

She hunched her shoulders and smiled. "I doubt it, but I can't say for sure. I only went inside it once with grandmother when I was a girl. She told me to take a good look at all the people and remember how desperate some of them looked. Then she never allowed me to enter it again. She said that gambling was one of the easiest ways to destroy people."

"And so you never went near?" he asked with a wicked smile. "Not even once as a small gesture of defiance?"

Lauren shook her head. "No. She was so wonderful, I didn't want to disappoint her."

"Disappointing people," he murmured after a noticeable silence. "The most painful of punishments." He sounded far away just then.

"Yes," she whispered.

"I happen to agree with you." Again she had the impression his thoughts were on something that brought him grief.

"Let's play over here." He gestured to the low-lying table in one corner of the sitting room. She sank down rather ungracefully into the cushions surrounding it. Rafi joined her with the ease and male agility of one who did this on a regular basis, extending his long powerful legs. Lauren tucked hers beneath her. The action brought her arm against his shoulder. Neither of them moved away.

He shot her a glance that seemed to be narrowed on her mouth. "Teach me how to play canasta."

Her body thrilled to the knowledge that he'd come with a pack of cards in order to spend more time with her. He pulled them from his trouser pocket and put them on the table. "They've already been shuffled."

"Good. I hate having to wait."

He laughed out loud, warming her clear through.

"Deal both of us fifteen cards," she instructed.

Her host took his time, smiling at her mysteriously as he did it.

Trying to ignore his dominating male aura she explained the rules of the game as clearly and concisely as she could.

He rubbed his thumb against his bottom lip in contemplation before moving the cards around in his hand. "Who taught you how to play?"

"Richard, my grandmother's husband."

They got started and she answered more questions as they went along. It didn't surprise her he had a razor-sharp brain plus a photographic memory. Once he'd caught on, they played until after midnight. The final count made her the overall winner by just a handful of points.

"I want a rematch," he growled the words, "but your eyelids are drooping so I'll say goodnight and we'll do this again tomorrow night."

She didn't know if she could live till then.

He left the cards on the table and got up in a lithe move. She clasped the hand he extended to her. "Oh—" she cried softly because the movement propelled her against him. "I'm sorry."

"I'm not." He rubbed his hands up and down her arms with growing urgency. "I've been waiting to do this all night. One little taste for a consolation prize, I think." The next thing she knew he kissed the nerve throbbing wildly at the base of her throat. Swarms of sensation filled her body, leaving her weak and trembling.

When she could lift her head, she saw fire blazing in the depths of those black eyes. "I'll come by for you at seven. If you're up to it, there's something I'd like to show you. We'll eat breakfast after that." Before she knew it, he'd slipped out of the suite.

Lauren glanced at her watch.

It was morning already.

Maybe she was in a dream. If she was, she never wanted to wake up. *Don't let me wake up. Please don't!*

Lauren prepared for bed quickly and set her watch alarm for six-thirty. She fell asleep at some point, but came awake a half hour before her alarm went off because she was so eager to see Rafi again.

After a shower and a hair wash, she dressed in tan pants and a white blouse, her uniform for the desert. At ten to seven, she heard a rap on the door before he entered the suite. He was early too, dressed like her. His piercing eyes traveled over her, causing every nerve ending to tingle.

"I like a woman who's punctual."

"That works both ways," she said, too breathlessly, as they walked along the passageway. She almost had to run to keep up with his long strides.

"Where are we going?"

"I'm anxious to show you the mews at the back of the palace where the royal falcons roost. I keep mine there. Johara loves a morning hunt. I've a feeling you'll enjoy watching her."

"You do falconry?"

"When I was young it was one of my favorite pastimes with my friends. These days I rarely have time for it." They went down a staircase and along another hall that eventually led to a shed-like room where she saw three falcons perched.

She watched as he moved over to one of the brownish birds, probably a foot and a half long from head to tail. The moment Rafi started speaking in Arabic, the bird cocked her head toward him.

He reached for a special glove on a nearby table. As soon as he put it on and held out his arm, she hopped on to it. Lauren would have given any-thing to have a camera to capture this splendid man interacting with a bird of prey equally noble.

She moved closer to them. "So *you're* one of Rafi's pets. You're magnificent." Just like your master. "Now I understand." The falcon tipped her head and regarded Lauren with a beady eye.

A slow smile broke the corners of Rafi's mouth. "Come with us, Lauren."

They walked outside into a world set aglow by

an early-morning sun. After the cold of the night, the heat was already building. A Jeep was parked nearby. He let his falcon fly. She rose high in the sky with shocking speed.

"Her wing span is huge!"

"Three feet to be exact. We'll follow her." His excitement was contagious. Lauren got in the Jeep with him and they headed out on a road that led toward the open desert.

"Johara will circle for food. If she can't find any, she'll come back to me."

She stared at his arresting profile. "Then what happens?"

"We'll drive her back to the mews where I'll make sure she's fed. The important thing is that she gets her exercise. When I can't do it, someone else sees to it the falcons fly at least two hours every day."

Lauren shielded her eyes. "Has she ever not come back and you had to go looking for her?"

He turned his head, meeting her eyes. "She

always comes back, but that's because I spent hours and hours training her in my late teens."

"Then she's old."

"Yes. I don't expect her to last much more than this season."

"Will you train a new falcon for yourself after that?"

"No. I'll never have that kind of time again," he answered in a voice that sounded so bleak, she couldn't account for it.

"Maybe if you have a child some day? A son or daughter who loves falconry as you do?"

In the next instant his countenance changed. An almost savage expression entered those incredible jet-black eyes, sending a chill that permeated her whole body. She wished she hadn't brought up something so personal.

"Forgive me if I've upset you." For no reason she could think of it hurt when it shouldn't have mattered at all.

He shot her a penetrating glance. "You've done nothing. We all have our own demons to battle from time to time. What do you say we enjoy the rest of the morning and see if Johara's old age has interfered with her ability to track down her prey? In her younger years she could spot it from a mile away."

The Jeep sped up. They'd left the road and were flying across the desert, which was flat in this part with some ground-cover vegetation. Ten minutes later they came upon a shelter which was nothing more than four poles holding up a canvas top. Beneath it she spotted chairs, and a table.

"We'll stop here for breakfast while we wait for Johara."

Lauren got out, delighted by the setup which included two thermoses of hot coffee and a supply of sandwiches and dates. Rafi appeared to have a fondness for them.

They ate with no time clock in mind. He answered her hunting questions with admirable patience. She satisfied his curiosity about her travels with her grandmother and Richard. The good times, the scary times—it didn't matter what they talked about. The sharing was what counted. The dark look she'd seen in his eyes earlier had vanished and Lauren knew instantly that she would clutch this memory to her forever.

The sun was almost overhead when she saw a speck in the sky. Rafi had seen it first because he'd started putting on his glove and walked outside to greet Johara. With great majesty his falcon circled him and then used her wings like a parachute, slowing her speed until she landed on the back of his wrist.

While he spoke in low tones to his bird, Lauren stood next to one of the poles, spellbound. "No luck today?" she eventually spoke.

Rafi shook his head, drawing her attention to his glossy black hair. "No, but there's always tomorrow. That's what I was telling her."

His tenderness with his pet reached a spot inside Lauren that gave her worlds of information about the kind of man Rafi was. She knew that there was no one in this world like him.

He walked over to the Jeep. After settling his bird on the back seat, he put a hood over her. "She feels safer like that." He satisfied Lauren's un-asked question, then flicked her a probing glance. "Shall we go? One of the staff will dismantle our restaurant."

She climbed in the front seat. "I've eaten in a lot of restaurants in my life, but I'll always con-sider this one my favorite." She didn't care if her voice wobbled from emotion. Lauren wanted him to know what this morning meant to her.

He reached for her hand and held on to it. "Even if it isn't true, I've decided I want to be-lieve you."

She pondered the strange remark all the way back to the mews. Of necessity he had to let go of her to carry his falcon inside, leaving her aching for his touch. After feeding the bird, they made their way back down the hallway and up the stairs.

Eventually they reached Lauren's suite. She dreaded this part because she knew he had his work to do and couldn't spend every minute of the day and night with her.

After opening the door, she turned to him. "Thank you for a wonderful outing, one I'll never forget."

He gazed at her through shuttered eyes. "Nor will I. Get some rest and I'll come by for you at six."

Joy.

Rashad left for his own suite, haunted by what was happening to him. Once he reached his own bedroom, he phoned his twin sister, Farah, and asked her to come to his suite the minute she was able. All three of his sisters were married, but it was Farah who had the most tender heart.

He didn't have to wait long before she swept into his sitting room. "Rashad?" She was wearing a rose caftan. Farah was a picture with her black hair hanging loose down her back, reminding him of the beauty of their women. Yet another image kept intruding of a female with spun-gold hair in enchanting disarray around her head and a complexion like strawberries in cream.

"Forgive me for bothering you, Farah."

"You're never a bother."

"Thank you for coming."

"You know I'd do anything for you." He knew it was true and loved her for it. She sat down on one of the chairs facing him. "Is this about our father? Is he worse?" Her dark eyes glinted with tears.

Their shape and color were different from the eyes he'd looked into out in the desert earlier. He'd had the sensation of stepping beyond the white froth of the surf where it broke into incredibly light-green water before melting into azure and then darkest blue.

"No. There's a guest here at the palace who was caught in a sandstorm two days ago. She almost didn't survive."

Farah cried out and put her hands to her mouth in horror.

"Dr. Tamam has assessed her and she's recovering well, but I think she might need a friend whilst she is here so she doesn't feel too alone. Her grandmother died recently. You're the perfect person to help her get through this difficult period. Would you be able to spend a little time with her this afternoon?"

"I'd be happy to do that. I'll do whatever I can to cheer her up. Where was she taken?"

"To the garden suite."

His sister rose to her feet. "You put her in there?" she asked incredulously. It was commonly known as the honeymoon suite for members of the royal family.

"I asked Dr. Tamam to take her there following the examination. After the horror of her experience, I thought she should be surrounded by beauty. Don't you agree?"

"Oh yes, of course! Only you would think of it. Who is she?"

"She's a young American woman, currently living in Switzerland, named Lauren Viret. She came here hoping to get over the sadness of losing the woman who raised her. Perhaps she'll tell you what it was she'd hoped to see and do while she was here at the Oasis. You're easy to talk to, Farah."

"I'll try, and you're right. She shouldn't be alone to dwell on that awful sandstorm."

"Thank you. You have my deepest gratitude for doing this personal favor for me. One more thing, I've told her I'm the head of palace security."

She smiled. "Well, I didn't think you'd tell her you were the prince."

"No. I thought the revelation might be too much for her and make her more uncomfortable about staying here. I told her to call me Rafi."

"I haven't heard you called that name in years." She winked at him before walking out to the corridor.

"Keep me updated, Farah. If she tells you anything I ought to know, come and tell me," he said as he followed her.

She kissed his cheek. "I promise."

He knew what was going through her head. In

another six months Rashad would be married. Eventually the day would come when he would have to obey his father and go through with the dreaded wedding ceremony that would bring an end to his freedom.

But while he was still single, his sister suspected him of having an interest in the American beyond concern for her comfort after her ordeal. That was exactly what Rashad wanted Farah to think. If she thought she could be an instrumental part of a passing romantic intrigue, so much the better. In her innocence, Farah made the perfect spy.

In the middle of her nap, Lauren heard the maid calling to her. She sat up on the bed where she'd been resting. "Yes?"

"You have a visitor, mademoiselle."

Lauren glanced at her watch. It was only four o'clock. Her pulse raced. Had Rafi come early to see her because he couldn't stay away? She slid off the bed. "Who is it?"

"The Princess Farah."

Princess?

Lauren put up a hand to muffle her cry, unable to believe her good luck. She'd come all this way to get information about her grandfather. So far she hadn't dared ask Rafi any questions about the royal family. As head of security he might suspect her motives, but who better than the princess herself? Surely she would enjoy talking of her family and its heritage?

"Have you shown her into the sitting room?"

"Yes, mademoiselle."

"Then please tell her I'll be with her in a moment."

She slipped on her sneakers and went to the bathroom to refresh her lipstick and brush her hair. Without wasting any time, she hurried into the other room. The princess, several inches taller than Lauren, stood near the desk dressed in cream pants and a stunning blood-red blouse. With a voluptuous figure and all that black hair piled on her head, she was the most striking woman Lauren had ever seen.

"Forgive me for keeping you waiting, Your Highness."

"Don't give it a thought, mademoiselle," Farah said in beautiful English. "My name's Farah. Rafi told me your name. May I call you Lauren? It's such a lovely name."

"Please," Lauren said, warming to her at once. "You have a beautiful name, too."

Her wide smile was enchanting. "Shall we sit down at the table? I asked for mint tea to be served in here."

"Thank you. This is a real honor for me." Lauren walked over to the table and sat down opposite her.

"The family heard about what happened to you during the sandstorm. I can't tell you how horrified I was when I learned of it." Tears glinted in her eyes. Even without them, Lauren felt her sincerity and it melted her on the spot. "It must have been awful for you."

"It was, but it's over now and I'm very grateful to be alive."

"My husband, Abdul, got caught in one when he was a boy. Sometimes I think maybe it's good he and I have not been blessed with children. If anything like that were to happen to them or to my husband again…" She couldn't finish the sentence.

"You must love your husband very much. Maybe one day you will be blessed with a child, too?"

"Abdul is the sweetest and kindest man I know, but sadly I have already suffered two miscarriages. The specialists I've seen cannot promise me anything and so we only hope…one day."

"I'm so sorry."

She shook her head. "Let's not talk about sad things. Instead we'll rejoice that you are alive. According to the doctor, you were close to death. He would have had to answer to my father if he hadn't brought you back to life."

Despite Rafi insisting it wasn't her appointed

time to die, Dr. Tamam had given her the medical treatment needed. "I'm very grateful to both Dr. Tamam and Rafi for everything they have done for me. If I could pay for the doctor's time perhaps or Rafi, who flew a helicopter to the accident scene and got me to the clinic in time."

"They don't want your money, Lauren. What's important is that you're all right."

"But to be the guest of the king…"

"My father welcomes all visitors if they come in peace."

If the king ever found out who Lauren really was, she would disturb his peace in ways she didn't dare think about. "Are you his only daughter?"

"No. I have two older sisters and a brother. He's my twin."

Lauren finished the sweet tea. "I would have loved brothers and sisters. Please convey my gratitude to your father and mother. I've never seen such a beautiful apartment in my life. The flowers on the patio are a miracle."

"My mother loves that garden."

"So do I."

"If you don't think it would tire you out, I'll be happy to show you around the palace grounds tomorrow. They're one big garden."

"I'd love that!" It might be her only chance to hear about Farah's family and learn something concerning her grandfather before she left the palace.

"Whatever else you would like to do while you're here at the Oasis, I'll arrange it."

Lauren's heart beat sped up. "You're very kind. Mustafa mentioned something about visiting the Garden of the Moon. Is it a place you think I should see?" Under the circumstances, she hoped the tiny white lie about Mustafa would be forgiven.

The Princess looked surprised. "I'm afraid it's not allowed."

Oh no. Quick. Think of something, Lauren.

"Between my inability to understand Arabic and his attempt to speak recognizable English, I obviously misunderstood him. It certainly doesn't matter."

"Perhaps he was talking about one of the specialty shops in the souk. Tourists love them."

"I'm sure I shall, too."

"I'll ring you tomorrow before I come for you."

CHAPTER FOUR

LATER that evening, Lauren left the bedroom, having dressed in a pair of cream-colored denims and a light-green blouse. As she entered the sitting room she heard Rafi's knock on the door before he entered wearing a dark silk shirt and dark trousers. He was the epitome of manhood. His name came out in a whisper.

"Good evening, Lauren. How did your day go?"

She smiled. "As if you didn't know. I was paid a visit by the Princess Farah. That was your doing, so don't deny it."

"I wasn't going to." He smiled back. "The day can hang heavy while you're recuperating alone."

"It went by fast for me. She's a lovely person. We had tea and biscuits. Tomorrow she's going to take me on a tour of the grounds." All the time she was talking, his eyes roamed over her face and figure, causing a suffocating feeling in her chest.

"Speaking of tours, I'm off duty now and thought you might like to see the main rooms of the palace. We'll eat dinner here in your room afterward."

Lauren closed her eyes tightly to catch her breath before opening them again. "I'd hoped to take a tour while I was visiting here."

He spread his hands in a way she was beginning to recognize as purely him. "Then I'm happy I can grant your wish. Perhaps your travel agency didn't know, but I've had to order the interior of the palace off limits to the public. In these modern times, there's too much danger to take risks."

She blinked. "I *didn't* know. If that sandstorm hadn't happened…"

Lines suddenly marred his handsome features. "Then we would never have met unless fate had deemed it otherwise. Shall we go?"

For the next hour Lauren wandered with him through room after room, marveling over the ancient citadel, which was a museum in and of itself. She wouldn't know where to begin describing the tiles on the floors and walls, the cutwork ceilings, the tapestries and urns, the sweeping staircases, all the trappings of a great empire.

In one of the great rooms, Rafi pointed out the lineage of the Shafeeq dynasty. Lining the walls were enormous framed oil portraits of the sheikhs. Each had a name plate, but Lauren couldn't read them. "What are their names?"

"You really want to know?"

"Yes. I think Arabic is a beautiful language. The names sound so different to my ear."

The comment seemed to please him. He turned to the portrait at the far end. With expert recall he gave her a short, stunning history of each one. In time they came to the second picture from the end.

"This one is Sheikh Malik Ghazi. The royal family calls him the great one."

Lauren's heart thudded painfully hard. It was almost impossible to believe she was standing in front of the likeness of her grandfather when he was maybe thirty years old. She'd already been given a description of him by her grandmother. The newspaper picture of him hadn't done him justice. He was everything Celia had said he was, and more.

Dark and splendid…like Rafi who had that same aura of authority, the fierce warrior look that could inspire followers and terrify their enemies. Lauren was furious with herself that she couldn't stop obsessing over this enigmatic man.

From the beginning he'd been careful to let her know he was still enjoying his bachelor status. One of these days soon she would have to leave the Oasis. For her own sake she didn't dare get in any deeper.

"Why did they call him that?"

"His father died young. King Malik had to take over the affairs of the kingdom at nineteen."

"That's too young to have such great responsibility, don't you think?" It was a miracle he'd had time for her grandmother.

"It is what it is."

Lauren had to smile at another one of those fatalistic comments she'd heard fall from his compelling lips. "I can't imagine it."

"He's the one who united many neighboring tribes and made our nation a greater kingdom than it was before."

Her mouth had gone so dry, she didn't know if she could enunciate clearly. "Is he still alive?"

"No. He died suddenly four months ago. Dr Tamam said his heart just stopped beating."

Celia had died a mere two months ago.

The timing of their deaths shook Lauren to the core. "How old was he when he passed away?"

"Eighty-one."

"Then he had a long full life, like Johara."

Quiet reigned before he nodded. "An astute observation."

"Is that how she'll die?"

"Maybe. I could hope she'll be in flight and

free when it happens. Birds weren't meant to be tamed."

"That's a surprising statement coming from you."

He flashed her a glance she couldn't decipher. "Lately I'm a mass of contradictions."

She sensed he didn't want to talk about it anymore and moved on to the last portrait. "I take it this is the king to whom I'm beholden beyond my ability to repay. King Umar Jalal Shafeeq," she said aloud. "I'm sorry for the bad pronunciation. His name and image were stamped on my entry visa."

"You said it well," he came back.

"I know he has a kind heart or I wouldn't be his guest. Is he a good king, too? You don't have to answer that if you can't, or don't want to."

A light flickered in Rafi's black eyes. "The world could learn from a leader like him."

Lauren's mother had been the king's half

sister… How sad they had never had a chance
to meet.

"Then he must be the best and you'll always
want to work for him." Lauren took a deep breath.
"Thank you for showing me this fabulous palace
and giving me this much of your time." She bit
her lip. "It's clear you're one of the king's right
hands, but you don't have to spend any more time
with me."

He angled his head toward her. "Lauren, do
I detect some fear that I'll beat you at cards tonight?"

"Yes," she lied, because being with him any
longer meant she might make a fool of herself
and do something with this man that she might
one day regret.

"Don't worry," he said with a devilish twist of
his lips. "If I win, I'll only take a few more bites
out of you." She could still feel his mouth against
her throat and Lauren's heartbeat increased to a
dangerous level.

When they reached her suite, their dinner had

been put on the low round table where they could eat and play cards at the same time. Rafi had thought of everything.

They sat down and got into the game in earnest, enjoying their food in between shuffles. In the end, she beat him again, this time by a much larger margin. Lauren decided he'd allowed her to win, but she didn't care. It was enough to be together and Lauren suddenly had the oddest sensation that it could go on forever.

He put the cards in a stack and shoved it to the center of the table. "Since you've won hands-down, what prize do you want from me?" Rafi reached for her hand and kissed the tips of her fingers. "Name it and it's yours." Shock waves traveled through her body.

"Do you think before I leave the Oasis it would be possible for me to visit the place where the sandstorm overtook the caravan?"

His brows formed a black bar above his eyes, changing the tenor of the evening. She wished now she hadn't brought it up. "Tell me, Lauren, why would you want to return to the spot that could only hold a devastating memory for you?"

"The maid has never found my medallion. Dr. Tamam said they made a search of the clinic, but it wasn't there. I think when Mustafa pulled me off the camel, he must have caused my chain to break and it's buried somewhere in the sand. I would give anything to recover it."

Rashad's dark head went back while he examined her features. "Don't you realize that if the medallion is out in the desert, it's buried beneath a mound of sand?"

"I'm sure you're right," she said in a subdued voice.

"You look tired," he said, helping her to her feet. "I'm going to say goodnight and will see you tomorrow." Instead of another bite from her throat, he kissed her forehead and disappeared so fast, she didn't have a chance to call him back.

She should have kept quiet about the medallion. Here he'd done everything humanly possible to make her happy since her accident, and she'd rewarded him by asking for another favor. In making that request, she'd stepped over a line. His swift departure left her under no delusions on that score. She wouldn't blame him if he thought she was the most selfish female alive.

Resolute, she sat down at the desk and composed a letter to the king, thanking him for his generous hospitality and the services of the clinic doctor and his chief of security. After that she wrote a note to Rafi.

When she'd finished, she put them outside the suite door, then walked over to the desk and dialed number one. A male voice came on the line. "This is Nazir. How may I help you, mademoiselle?"

"Forgive me for bothering you this late, but I'd like to leave the palace in the morning and I need a driver to take me to a hotel. Could you arrange that for me?"

"Of course. I will send someone to your room after you've been served your breakfast."

"Thank you very much. One more thing. There

are two letters outside my door. Would you make certain they are delivered?"

"Certainly."

She hung up the phone, wishing the travel agency she'd called in Montreux would ring her back. They'd promised to arrange for helicopter transportation for her from Al-Shafeeq to El-Joktor and would phone her with the details.

Lauren had come here with questions about her grandmother and the romance she had encountered with Malik. But now she had seen firsthand how captivating this desert kingdom was. She might not have answers to all her questions, but she knew one thing for sure. She needed to get away from the man who had captured her own heart; she needed to get away from Rafi.

Rashad had just gotten off the phone with Farah when Nazir came to his suite with two envelopes and informed him Mademoiselle Viret wished to leave the palace in the morning. That didn't surprise him.

He told Nazir he'd take care of it. After he left, Rashad stood in the middle of his sitting room and opened the envelope addressed to his father first. After reading it, he turned to the one meant for him.

Dear Rafi,
Princess Farah said neither you or Dr. Tamam wanted payment for your actions during the sandstorm. I'm left with no choice but to simply thank you for saving my life. I'll never forget you.
Lauren.

Her sentiment worked both ways. Rashad had wanted her so much tonight, he'd felt as though he was dying. He'd never known hunger like this before. It went beyond the physical to some other place, sending the same kind of shivers racing across his bronzed skin he'd felt when he'd picked her up in his arms the first time.

That same chemistry had been instantaneous

for her, too. He remembered the second she'd awakened to discover him holding her hand at the bedside. She hadn't spoken for a long time. That was because a white-hot heat more blazing than the desert sun had enveloped them through no volition of their own. The harder they'd fought it, the more intense their desire had grown.

Though he believed she had an agenda, no human could simulate the chemistry between them. Tonight those heavenly green eyes had seduced him, willing him to make love to her.

Throughout his life he'd known temptation and had been able to withstand it because he was his father's son and had a sacred duty to uphold. If he hadn't been careful all these years, he would be dead by now. His father had trusted no one and neither did he, least of all this beautiful flesh-and-blood creature with flaxen hair and peridot eyes sent to weaken his defenses.

And he knew she'd been sent.

Tonight Farah had phoned and given him the proof. At first he'd thought she hadn't told him anything that could help him. By the tone of Farah's voice, Rashad thought Lauren had won his sister over completely. Just when he'd decided Farah hadn't discovered anything that could help him, she'd mentioned the Garden of the Moon.

That was the clue he'd been waiting for. Every alarm in Rashad's hard body had gone off. He'd found a link to the medallion and was getting closer to an answer.

Wasting no time, he'd phoned Mustafa who had sworn an oath he'd never said anything about the Garden of the Moon to Mademoiselle Viret. According to him, the foreigner had been unusually quiet and had appeared deep in thought throughout the entire journey.

Rashad believed him.

He finally went to bed, determined that over the next few days he would get a confession out of her, starting by giving her what she wanted first.

"Good morning, mademoiselle. I'm Nazir." The fortyish-looking man stood in the doorway wearing traditional Arab robes. He broke into a smile. "We spoke on the phone last night, but haven't yet met. I've been instructed to accompany you to the western gate."

"Thank you for coming. Did you get the letters?"

"Yes. They've been delivered."

So fast? "Excellent. Well, I'm ready." She started to pick up her suitcases, but he said, "Leave them in here."

Lauren frowned. "Leave them? I don't understand."

He spread his hands. "All will be explained if you will accompany me."

This meant Rafi had gotten her note and knew of her plans. As head of security, nothing went on in the palace he didn't know about. "Very well."

Once out the door she followed Nazir along one corridor and down another she hadn't seen before. The palace was like a small city. Eventually they came to a portico and he led her beyond it to a glorious garden of palms and desert plants growing outside the palace.

Nazir made a gesture with his hands. "This way, please."

Several hundred yards off in the distance she spied a helicopter gleaming in the sun. She walked toward it, curious to know what was going on. Closer now she saw three men inside, one at the controls. Another one jumped down wearing tall leather boots.

There was no mistaking Rafi in a khaki shirt and trousers. She didn't like admitting it, but just seeing his burnished face and those strong hands on his hips in a totally male stance sent an explosion of excitement through her body. It wasn't fair for one man to be that endowed. She'd hoped to put distance between them, but such wasn't the case.

"How are you this morning, Lauren?"

"I'm fine, thank you."

"We'll see." He moved closer, pressing the back of his hand to her cheeks and forehead. After receiving her note, he could be excused for wondering why she'd made plans to leave the palace without telling him last night.

His touch electrified her, never mind his black eyes that reduced her insides to pulp. "I—I don't have a fever," her voice faltered.

"Let me be the judge of that," came his answer in a smoky tone. He wasn't talking about the state of her health. With a comment like that, Lauren wasn't sure if her legs would hold her up.

"Are you satisfied?"

"I guess I'll have to be," he murmured. "If you're still intent on visiting the site of the sandstorm, the king has put a pilot at your disposal."

Her debt to the king continued to grow, but of course it was Rafi who made things happen. "I shouldn't have said anything to you last night. You've all done more than enough for me."

"It won't take long. Have you flown in a helicopter before?"

"Yes. Many times, in fact."

"Then let's be off. Just remember we're flying

to the sun's anvil. It'll be 122 degrees Fahrenheit, if not more, so beware."

On that note he helped her inside. His hands rested on her hips longer than necessary before she climbed in the back and strapped herself in the seat. It was all she could do not to turn around and launch herself into his arms.

The man next to her in Arab dress smiled at her. He had to have noticed what had transpired while Rafi was assisting her.

This was madness. Shame over her desire for him drove her to keep her eyes trained on the desert. The rotors whined. When liftoff occurred, she didn't once look ahead to where she'd be able to see the back of his head.

Instead she stared out her window and watched as the palace and finally the small green settlement of the Oasis itself disappeared. It was almost frightening to see nothing but sand below, an entirely different perspective from the air than on the ground.

They flew on into a world of nothing but undulating sand dunes forming their own fantastically shaped hills and valleys, untouched except for scorching sun and air. Out in this vast expanse, you had no sense of direction but for the sun which was almost at its zenith, denoting noon.

The pilot knew where they were, with today's technology, he could pinpoint the exact spot where the sandstorm had come upon her caravan. The real marvel were the Bedouins of the desert who'd been crossing these sands for millennia and had their own ways of functioning day and night in such an inhospitable wilderness. Yet for all that it had a terrifying beauty.

No sign of brown mountains sweeping across the horizon like a tsunami today. Maybe Rafi had been right and it hadn't been her appointed time to die. Instead fate had delivered her into his arms. She closed her eyes, trying to shut out her thoughts of him, but it did no good.

From the first moment she'd heard his deep voice and had felt his hand swallow hers—

even before she saw him—she'd *felt* him to her very soul.

"Lauren? We've arrived."

At the sound of his voice, she let out a little cry of surprise and opened her eyes. She'd been so buried in her own torturous thoughts, she hadn't realized they'd landed.

"If you're feeling unwell, we'll return to the palace." What made him think there was something wrong? She didn't understand.

He opened the door and got out. When she climbed forward, he put an impersonal hand on her upper arm to assist her as she jumped into the sand, but an electric current ran through her body just the same. They'd landed in a valley with gigantic mounds of sand spreading in every direction. The pilot stayed at the controls. The other man climbed out and walked a distance off.

Stunned to be that little granule of sand again, she looked all around before flicking Rafi a glance. "Where did it happen exactly?"

"According to the pilot, beneath this mound in

front of you. I flew your body from here to the palace in the hope you could be revived."

She gasped because the sand dune in front of her rose at least twenty feet. Its smooth crescent shape ran the length of the horizon. Lauren took several steps forward, but with each thrust, her foot sank and it took effort to pull it out.

How foolish of her to think she could come out here and find anything, let alone her medallion! It was buried here somewhere, forever. The knowledge seemed to bring an end to an era for Lauren.

Her grandmother, her grandfather, the medallion—all were gone. The end of the beginning or the beginning of the end? Whatever, it was written in the sand now.

Her shoulders started to shake as tears began falling. She hung her head because she was beginning to sound like Rafi. She needed to get out of here and start a new life for herself, maybe in America? Wherever, she knew she needed to be somewhere far away from everything that re-minded her of the past, away from *him*.

She felt him approach her side. Her body came alive whenever he was around and the sensations were so new, so different that they upset her. She didn't know where to go with her new feelings for him. "You warned me, Rafi, but please don't say anything. I only need five more minutes."

The suffocating air was so hot that the moisture evaporated as it dripped off her chin. Though he obeyed her, he didn't go away. Instead he wrapped his arms around her neck from behind so the tears fell on his bronzed skin. He pressed his chin in her hair and drew her into him in a protective gesture where she felt the steady pounding of his heart against her back.

For the moment he was comforting her like he might a child. Unfortunately the warmth from his hard-muscled body and his great strength increased her desire for him. She'd known such desire existed after listening to her grandmother, but she'd never felt its power until now.

This physical thing between them was sublime torture for her, tapping into her deepest emotions. She couldn't hold back the tears. They burst over the dam. How long she sobbed, she didn't know. Twice now she'd fallen apart in his arms.

She couldn't fathom leaving him and this place where life and death had taken on an entirely new meaning. Her grandmother had been faced with the same decision, but somehow she'd found the will to walk away from King Malik.

How did she do that?

Lauren didn't have Celia's resolve. Never to see Rafi again…

Ashamed because she was making a spectacle of herself, she sniffed hard and moved out of his arms to walk back to the helicopter on her own. This time it was the other man who helped her inside. She thanked him and the pilot before Rafi climbed in and shut the door.

Once more they were off, winging through the sky with no trace of clouds. Nothing but hot, hot blue, the sun reflecting off the sand sculptures below and the haunting profile of a man who was larger than life to her. *Larger than her grandmother's sheikh*. For the rest of Lauren's days, that picture would remain indelibly carved on her consciousness.

The men talked back and forth. She noticed Rafi speaking into his headset. Lauren could imagine that they had much more to do with their time than ferry around the American who must appeared spoiled to them, but as she was a guest of the king, they had their orders. When she got back to the palace, she intended to stay in her room for the rest of the day.

Rafi put out a hand to help her down from the helicopter. "Enjoy your afternoon. We'll talk later," he said before walking swiftly away in another direction, taking her heart with him. Nazir stood by to escort her back to the palace.

Now that another duty was done, Rafi could get back to his job as head of security. That was as it should be, she told herself, but her pain at watching him disappear sent her on a churning, downward spiral as she followed Nazir along various corridors.

She thought they looked different from the other ones. Before she could question him, Princess Farah came out of a set of doors wearing riding clothes. She smiled at Lauren.

"I'm so glad you are back. I just returned from a horseback ride with my husband, come inside and have a swim with me. We'll eat lunch by the pool."

"That sounds lovely, but I didn't bring a suit."

"I have many I haven't even worn." She glanced at Nazir. "Thank you for finding her." He said something back in Arabic and walked away.

They entered a fabulous octagonal room with a round swimming pool and a high ceiling of fretwork and inlaid tiles. "You were looking for me?"

"Yes. I thought you might like to go riding with me, but found out you'd already left your suite."

"Your father arranged for me to fly out to the place where the sandstorm hit."

The princess looked shocked. "Why would you want to do that?"

"It sounds silly now, but I lost a piece of jewelry my grandmother gave me when the sandstorm hit, and I hoped I might see it in the sand. Rafi told me it would be buried. Of course, he was right."

Farah's liquid dark eyes were filled with compassion. "I'm so sorry, but compared to your life, something material isn't so important in the scheme of things."

"You're right, Your Highness." It belonged to the past.

The princess smiled and showed Lauren to an anteroom where she could change. When she came out again in a yellow bikini, she discovered they had company. Farah made the introductions.

Of the three black-haired sisters, Lauren found herself staring at the eldest, Samira, who had the look of Lauren's mother. Samira was forty-one with five children. She'd brought her two youngest to the pool, an eight-year-old son and a five-year-old daughter.

Of course, she was older now than Lauren's mother had ever been. Still, Samira reminded her of some of the pictures in her wallet of Lana, and it gave Lauren's heart a tug to see the resemblance.

Basmah was thirty-nine and had four children. She'd brought along her youngest twin daughters, just turning four.

Farah explained that she and her twin brother Rashad were both thirty-four. Lauren saw the longing and love in Farah's eyes whenever she looked at her nieces and nephews. They were all adorable and got in the pool with Lauren without hesitation.

After some serious playtime, she climbed out and joined the others. They lay on loungers by the side of the pool to keep their eye on the children. Lauren sipped on her iced fruit drink. Having been born princesses, all three women were the products of formal education and spoke excellent English. Lauren discovered they were well-traveled and forward-thinking about their nation's future.

Their conversation was focused fairly constantly on their brother Rashad, a chemical engineer who'd been doing great things at his lab in Raz to open up new industries. Basmah and Samira were helping their mother plan the thirty-fifth birthday party for Farah and her brother being held in another week. The lot fell to Farah to think of a birthday present they could give him. Something exceptional.

"What do you think, Lauren?"

"Well, if I had a brother, I'd find him something to enjoy when he wants to relax."

Basmah shook her head. "He doesn't know how to relax."

"She's right!" Samira echoed. "He's too busy working all the time."

"Surely he has down time."

"If he's not at work, he's off on his horse," Farah inserted.

"He likes them better than women," Basmah added. "At least that's what all his girlfriends say."

Everyone laughed, including Lauren. "In that case, why not pick out a fine saddle blanket?"

"For that matter, why not a new saddle?"

Lauren eyed Samira. "You could give him one, but he probably won't use it."

She frowned. "Why not?"

"Because it needs to fit him and his horse like a glove. No hand fits a glove the same way, neither does a man on his horse. I bet it took your brother a long time to decide on the one he uses now."

Farah nodded. "You're right. Abdul would say the same thing."

"Does he like jewelry? Maybe you could give him a ring from all of you with three stones."

"That's a lovely idea, Lauren, but he doesn't like them. He says they irritate him when he works."

"Well, he'll have to get used to one when he's married," Basmah commented.

"He's dreading that day."

Lauren looked at Farah. "In this day and age he still can't choose his own wife?"

She shook her head. "No. It's tribal law that our father chooses the spouses, I'm glad he picked Abdul for me. I love him now. But it's different for you, being an American."

"That's true. Even if my father were alive, a woman still gets to pick the man she will marry."

Lauren felt Basmah's eyes on her. "You are the most beautiful American woman I ever saw in my life. When you go back to your country, you will have many opportunities to marry and do your own choosing."

"Thank you for the compliment, but the truth is, I don't plan to marry."

"You don't want children?" Farah cried.

Lauren saw one of the little twins running along the tiles to catch up with her sister. She was so sweet. "Not without the right man."

"He exists somewhere," Farah said with her heart in her eyes. "You have to believe that."

"I do," Lauren said with a sad smile, "but it doesn't mean fate will bring us together." Rafi's image would always be sketched on her heart.

"That is true," Samira murmured. "You sound very wise."

Lauren shook her head. If she'd been wise, she wouldn't have come to the desert, but then she wouldn't have met these delightful women who were also the grandchildren of King Malik. She wouldn't have met Rafi.

"You don't know how lucky you are," Farah confided. "I worry about our brother who will have to live with a woman he doesn't love. They'll be married at the end of the year."

"Give them time," Samira counseled.

"Time won't fix anything for Rashad," Farah blurted. "I know my twin brother too well. He'll never be happy. Our mother's fears have come true, he has been too favored."

"What do you mean?" Lauren questioned her.

Farah spread her hands. "He's been given every gift a man can have. Our mother is afraid there'll be a price to pay."

"A price?"

"Yes. Heaven is jealous of him."

"Our mother worries too much," Basmah said.

Farah looked sad. "I happen to agree with her. Something will come along that Rashad will want more than anything on earth, and for all his godlike virtues, it won't be granted."

Godlike. Celia's very words. They raised goosebumps.

With nothing but the sound of the childrens' voices in the background, the women grew quiet. Their collective silence indicated they feared Farah had spoken the truth. How awful for their brother.

Before long the children grew restless and the fun ended. Everyone left the pool room except for Farah. "Perhaps later in the week you'll come to my suite and have dinner with me."

"What about your husband?"

"He's away on business and won't be back until next week."

"Then I'd like that very much."

"So would I. I'll phone you."

Lauren left the pool and headed for her suite. She'd just returned to her room where a dinner tray was waiting for her when the phone rang. It set off her pulse because she'd been hoping to hear from Rafi. She picked up and said hello, trying not to sound too eager.

"Mademoiselle Viret? This is Louis at the travel office in Montreux."

"Oh—thank you for returning my call," she said, fighting her disappointment. "Have you made new travel arrangements for me?" She was determined to leave the Oasis before…before she could no longer do so.

"*Desolé, mademoiselle*. I'm most sorry to tell you that it will be impossible for you to leave Al-Shafeeq until the date you'd originally set to return to El-Joktor."

She panicked. "But I told you I'd pay you extra."

"I'm afraid it's not a question of money. The men in charge of the caravans don't operate by the same rules as most of us. They agree on a fee and a time when they're ready to go. You can try another agency, but I can promise you won't have better luck with them."

"I believe you. Then I'll book a helicopter."

"There is no service at the Oasis except in an emergency, and it has to be cleared through the royal palace. The fee would be prohibitive."

That meant going through Rafi. She couldn't possibly ask him for another favor that would require the king's involvement. "I understand. *Merci, Louis.*"

With a growing sense of inevitability, she hung up the receiver. There was going to be no escape until Mustafa took her back to El-Joktor. Since she was a guest of the king, she couldn't go to a hotel. That would be an insult to him. But another night with Rafi, let alone another week, would melt her resolve not to get any more involved.

She ate part of her dinner, wondering if he

would call or come by. Maybe she'd watch TV; she moved over to the sofa facing the cabinet holding it. With the aid of the remote, she surfed a few channels, all in Arabic. Everything reminded her of Rafi. She shut it off and rested her head on the pillow while tears slipped out beneath her eyelids.

What other man could ever cause her to burn with desire the way he did? He brought her to life in a way that frightened her because she knew no other man could ever make her feel that way again. This morning she'd been wrapped in his arms. She'd felt the essence from his soul reach out and fill hers. For a little while they'd stood in the sand dunes, one pulsating entity.

Lauren couldn't comprehend not ever seeing him again and in that moment she knew that she was falling in love with him.…

Conflicted beyond bearing, Rashad returned from Raz at dinnertime, barely able to function. Taking Lauren to the desert earlier in the day hadn't shed any new light on her secret. Worse, her tears had brought out his protective instincts. He'd come close to breaking every self-imposed rule by kissing her senseless in front of the pilot and bodyguard.

He'd never believed in witches until now, but she was a temptress, a beauty who didn't seem to know it, a spy who didn't spy, a flirt who didn't flirt, a seducer who'd made no move to seduce. She was the sweet embodiment of the word *treachery* in breathtaking female form. At this point he was ready to carry her off and forget the world.

To his dismay, she'd claimed all his attention for the last three days. During that time he hadn't checked in with his father who liked daily updates on business. Rashad needed to drop in on him now before he went to her room.

"At last, Rashad." His father was sitting in a chair with his sore foot resting on the ottoman while he drank his favorite mint tea. "I've had dinner, but I'll ask for a tray to be sent up for you."

"Thank you, but I ate earlier." Rashad sat on the seat opposite his father. "I was in Raz until a half hour ago and came as soon as I could."

"I'm glad you're here because there's something important I need to talk to you about."

An odd nuance in his father's tone made Rashad uneasy. "What is it?"

"I've had correspondence with Sheikh Majid al Din. He wants to move up your wedding date."

Rashad shot out of the seat, turning away from his father while he attempted to contain his shock and yes, *anger*. He'd been dreading this since his sixteenth birthday.

"I can see this has upset you." His father had always been kind to him. His voice was kindness itself right now, but Rashad couldn't handle it.

"By how much?" he asked through clenched jaws.

"He wants to see his daughter married in a month."

"A *month?*"

His father eyed him with love. "I've touched the only sore spot in you."

Rashad stopped pacing. "I knew this day was coming, but I thought I had more time. I need a moment to take in the realization that my world is about to change."

"I felt the same way when your grandfather confronted me. He told me who my bride would be two years before my wedding. I decided to lessen your pain by only giving you a month to agonize about the coming ceremony."

The irony of those words would have made Rashad break out in harsh laughter if he didn't love his father so much. "Have you told anyone else?"

"No one except for Nazir who has been our go-between. I'm to let Sheikh Majid know in three days' time if this is satisfactory. This thing has to be done in absolute secrecy so as not to upset the neighbors on our other borders."

"Not even my sisters know?" Rashad persisted

He shook his head. "Especially not Farah, who continually begs me to let you choose the woman you will marry. She wearies me with it."

"Farah believes in love," Rashad muttered.

His father grunted. "You and I know that a powerful kingdom cannot be ruled by a sheikh who is so besotted with his wife, he can't see the shadows of his enemies outside the tent."

The palace was hardly a tent, but Rashad understood the point of the metaphor well enough. It had been drummed into his head since he was a child. His father would be horrified to know that a possible enemy had already invaded the palace and, as yet, Rashad had done nothing about it!

The way his father talked, Rashad was convinced that his sister had said nothing about the American woman staying at the palace. Was it simply coincidence Sheikh Majid wanted to speed up the time? Or could it be some grand design to help Rashad fight the spell this woman had cast over him?

It *was* a spell. How else to explain the weakness

he felt for her, the longing that kept him in pain throughout the night. Could she truly be like the female black widow he and his young friends had once watched in fascination while she stung her mate to death?

Tonight he would get the truth out of her. His hell had gone on long enough. Once she was exposed, his desire for her would turn to bitter gall. It had to. "If you'll forgive me, father, I need to be alone so I'll say goodnight."

"I understand that better than you do. Goodnight, my son."

Once out the door, Rashad checked the phone logs in the communications room. Nothing had turned up on their guest except for two short calls to and from the travel agency in Switzerland.

With everything taken care of for the moment he strode down the hall swiftly to reach the other side of the palace. His wedding day had been moved forward, but tonight he didn't want to think about it. He wanted Lauren.

Right now he was the one who felt closed in.

He craved a night with her where he could pretend he was a free man like any other, able to be with the woman he desired. For tonight he would forget his royal responsibilities. Until she'd been blown in to his world, he'd never felt or resented them so heavily.

At Ziyad's place he could be himself. No one would bother him or give away his identity. Tonight it was crucial he acted on the feelings roiling inside him. What made it more exciting was that despite the part she'd been playing from the beginning, he knew Lauren desired him, too. In fact, every word and gesture was putting an edge on their experience, heightening the potent tension between them.

After knocking on her door, he slipped inside and discovered her on the sofa in front of the television. When he walked around in front of her, he saw moisture on her cheeks and didn't know what to think.

"How is it that more often than not, I find you in tears?"

CHAPTER FIVE

LAUREN'S cry filled the room. She lifted her head and sat up, pushing the tendrils of silky hair out of her face. *"Rafi—"* Her voice throbbed.

He knelt down next to her, all male and warm. She could smell his aroma. The scent from his shower was familiar to her now. His piercing black eyes roved over her flushed face with relentless scrutiny. "Are you still so sad?"

"I've just been thinking about my grandmother this evening. I guess it's a case of knowing that when I get home, I'll have to deal with my life on my own. As you can see, I'm a c-coward," she stammered and wiped the moisture off her face. "How was your day?"

Shadows had darkened his features. "I'd rather not talk about it." He took hold of her hand and smoothed his thumb over her wrist. "Naturally you feel closed in, so how about we go out tonight? We'll go to a local cabaret with music and dancing. I'm off duty. Here in the desert we believe music helps dispel sadness. Does that appeal to you?"

"It sounds wonderful."

"Good. While you freshen up, I'll do the same and come by for you in ten minutes." He got to his feet. "Don't forget to bring a wrap, it will be cool out."

"What should I wear?"

"The outfit you have on is perfectly adequate, but if you wish to change, that's up to you."

She watched him leave, but she had no intention of going out with him in pants and a top. After deciding the black was too dressy, she decided on her cream-colored dress. She put it on over her head and pulled the hem down to her knees. The sleeveless cotton outfit more or less skimmed her body. An insert of cream lace formed the neckline.

She only had one pair of high heels, black. After slipping them on, she put on lipstick and brushed her hair, then reached for her black sweater. By the time she heard his voice coming from the sitting room, her excitement at going out with him was so great, it sent her heart tripping off the charts.

To her embarrassment she almost *ran* into the other room, leaving him to believe she couldn't wait to be with him. With her face hot, she stared at the tall, striking, black-haired man standing there in beige trousers and a black silk shirt.

"You look lovely." His deep voice resonated through her body.

She could hardly talk. "Thank you." There were no words to describe his masculine appeal.

Between his lashes, his black eyes gleamed. "Shall we go?"

They left the suite and walked down several long hallways to a palace entrance in companionable silence. Though their bodies never touched, Lauren felt the electricity between them like a living thing. She stepped outside into a garden of palms where the last stages of twilight could be seen through the fronds. The perfumed air was still hot.

He took her sweater before helping her into the waiting black limo, evidently a privilege he enjoyed due to his position at the palace. Their arms brushed. The touch of silk against her bare arm left her trembling with unassuaged needs.

Lauren was so aware of him, she scarcely noticed where they were driving. Before she knew it, they slowed down and stopped in front of a restaurant with a bistrolike facade. She heard Arabic music before he escorted her through a doorway of beads to the dark, smoke-filled interior.

The place was filled with locals and a few tourists. They were seated at small square tables surrounding a dance floor with a band playing in the background. A heavyset man at the bar nodded to him and indicated an empty table beneath a balcony that ran along one side. No sooner had he seated her than a waiter came over.

Rafi flicked her a probing glance. "What is your pleasure?"

"A cola."

"Nothing stronger?"

"Not tonight."

"So be it." He said something to the other man in Arabic, then moved his chair next to her and put his arm around the back of hers. His closeness sent a wave of delight through her body. "You're about to see one of our women belly dance," he spoke next to her ear, disturbing her hair. "If she dances for me, it will be to make you jealous because you're the most beautiful woman in the room."

Lauren smiled and lifted her eyes to him. "How many times have you made *her* jealous by coming in here with one of your favorites?"

The waiter returned with two colas, followed by fanfare from the band, saving him from answering.

A woman close to forty, and built along the lines of Farah, undulated onto the dance floor. Her loose black hair swung back and forth below her waist with hypnotic rhythm while her stomach and hips did the most amazing things.

As Lauren looked around, she noticed that most of the audience was made up of men. This close to the woman, Lauren could understand their fascination. She danced with enough seductive expertise to restart a heart that had gone into cardiac arrest.

Lauren cast a covert glance at Rafi whose gaze was riveted on the desert beauty with her red lips and flashing black eyes. Her spangles and bracelets made their own brand of music. The woman worked the floor. Near the end of her routine, she approached their table.

The dancer flashed Lauren a look that could kill before her gaze settled on Rafi. While she put on a show for him alone, bending backward to give him a good long look at her, Lauren saw unfeigned desire in the woman's eyes. It was so blatant, Lauren looked down. When the music ended, the dancer didn't move away.

He said something to the woman. She backed away slowly. But at the last moment before she disappeared, she shot Lauren a look of venom. Lauren grabbed her glass and drank all her cola at once.

The second she put her empty glass on the table, she heard the band start to play a song she could identify. Rafi stood up. "Let's dance."

In a euphoric daze, Lauren moved into his strong arms. She'd been in them before, but this time it was different. He held her so close, she could feel his hard-muscled body down to their feet. There was no place to put her arms but around his neck. As she did so, she felt his hands rove over her back and pull her up tight against him.

"It's a good thing we're surrounded by people. Otherwise I would devour you," he admitted with a frankness that caught her off guard. "Have I frightened you?" he whispered against her lips.

"No." Her voice throbbed, she needed him the way she needed air to breathe.

"That's good because I'm going to kiss you. It's something I've wanted to do since the moment you woke up after the sandstorm." So saying, his compelling mouth closed over hers.

At the first taste of him, the room, the music, the people…everything faded into nothingness. All she was aware of was this man who'd set her on fire. She didn't know where one hungry kiss ended and another one began. Filled with indescribable ecstasy, she never wanted this rapture to stop.

Her grandmother had prophesied it. With the right man, the passion in Lauren would be unleashed. She knew now her whole life had been waiting for Rafi who'd brought her to life and was making her feel immortal. *Malik's words*. Like grandfather, like granddaughter.

A groaning protest escaped her swollen lips when he suddenly relinquished her mouth and put his hands on her upper arms to separate her from him. She watched him swallowing hard. His breathing sounded shallow. "We have to leave," he said in a husky voice.

Lauren couldn't bear it, but when she saw everyone in the candlelit room looking at them, she realized she'd been so enthralled, she'd forgotten where they were. Another belly dance was about to begin. Lauren needed no more urging and hurried outside ahead of him.

She climbed into the waiting limo without his help. When he got in, he sat opposite her. The car started moving. He eyed her for a long moment. "I'm not going to apologize for what happened in there."

"Did I ask you to?" she cried. "I'm the one who practically threw myself at you. Obviously it shouldn't have happened, so please—let's not get into a dissection of my emotional lapse."

They rode back to the palace in a silence punctuated with her heart pounding out an irregular rhythm. It would never go back to normal. When they arrived at the entrance, she grabbed her sweater lying on the seat and took off, anxious to reach her suite. Halfway down the first hall, his long strides caught up to her.

She kept going and soon arrived at her destination. He followed her inside the doors. Without closing them he said, "I'll say goodnight. In the morning after breakfast, Nazir will come for you and show you out to the limo where I'll meet you."

Her hands made a fussing movement. "Won't you have to be on duty?"

"I'm making the time for you."

His words made her body go weak. "Thank you for taking me out tonight. I loved it, even if the dancer wanted to kill me."

"I believe she did. What's interesting is that all the males in the room wanted to kill me. Goodnight."

To Rashad's chagrin, the night turned out to be an endless one. After getting up, he paced the tiles, counting the minutes until he could be with her again. When it was time, he dressed in a non-royal Bedouin robe and sunglasses.

Her eyes exploded like green fire when he slid into the back of the limo next to her a few minutes later. She wore tan pants and a white top. Her fragrance was always a feminine assault on his senses.

"Good morning." He kissed the corner of her mouth because he couldn't help himself and felt her quiver. Their desire for each other was tangible. "I thought you might like to go shopping in the souk. You'll need a translator, so I'm offering my services." He clasped the hand nearest him and heard her take a deep breath.

The Oasis, a three by five mile rectangle, contained the village where he'd taken her last night. In no time at all they reached the center. He told the driver to drop them in front of the Almond Tree Café and wait for them.

She put on a pair of sunglasses and got out after he'd helped her. Together they started moving among the locals. A few tourists were about.

They walked in front of the shops in the bazaar. With her blond hair and fair complexion, not to mention her enchanting figure, she was a target for every eye.

Enough items were displayed to please the typical tourist. Though she moved slowly and inspected everything, she didn't buy anything. "If there's something that catches your eye, I'll barter a good price for you."

"Thank you, but I just like to look." They eventually turned a corner. Halfway down she paused. "Oh good. A bookstore." After going inside, she asked in English if the owner had a book in Arabic on the Shafeeq dynasty. The old man didn't understand.

Rashad's brows met. She wanted a book on his family? That made no sense to him. "Maybe I can help. What kind of book do you mean?"

She turned to him. "Any literature on the Shafeeq family. Something I can take home as a souvenir."

There wasn't such a thing in the public domain,

but she didn't know that. He asked the owner in Arabic. The old man shook his head before breaking into a long explanation.

Rashad translated for the owner. "Would you like a cigar box with a likeness of Sheikh Umar or Sheikh Malik on the top?"

A genuine look of excitement broke out on her face. "I'd love both of them! How much does he want for them?"

"I'll get the price down for you."

"No—" She put a hand on his arm. "He has to earn a living."

When Rashad told her the notated price, she signed one of her traveler's checks that paid him three times the amount. It brought a broad smile to the man's face. He put the boxes in a sack for her.

"Is this the extent of your shopping spree?" he teased.

She chuckled. "Yes."

"Then let's walk back to the Almond Tree for a juice drink."

"I could use one of those."

Rashad thanked the owner. He caught hold of her hand once more and they made their way through the village like a married couple. By the time they returned to the palace, the sense of belonging to her was so strong he could taste it, and he tightened his grip.

This would be what it was like if he could have a normal life with her. They could live and love to their hearts' content, sharing all those little things lovers did with no fear of it coming to an end.

A month.

With the sand in the hourglass steadily emptying into the bottom half, each minute meant he was drawing closer to the time when there'd be no more happiness.

He left her at the door to her suite, telling her he'd get in touch with her later because duty called. She eyed him soulfully with those gorgeous green eyes before closing the door. As it

clicked, he fought to repress a curse that thi...
thing had happened to him.

Torment didn't begin to describe his emotions.
Despite the mystery he hadn't solved, he still
had the medallion in his possession so she would
not be able to use it against his family. What he
should do was have her flown to El-Joktor today.

Nazir could accompany her and personally
escort her onto a jet headed for Geneva. If she
ever tried to come back, she would discover all
borders to his kingdom were permanently closed
to her. Knowing she was barred from Rashad's
sight, he might be able to bear going through with
his nuptials.

But what if he couldn't?

Terrified of that answer, he rushed back to his
suite, needing to act. He looked around the apartment as if he might find a magic solution to his
turmoil. There was none. What kind of a son was
he? What kind of a king would he make if a soft
traitorous woman with bewitching green eyes
and golden hair could reduce him to this state?

At war with himself, he fought the battle for a few more minutes before he picked up the receiver of his land line. Forcing himself to speak, he called the airport in El-Joktor and booked a one-way flight to Geneva for one passenger.

Determined as he'd never been in his life, he rang his mechanic and asked that a helicopter and pilot from his father's fleet be ready for flight within the hour. Finally he phoned Nazir and asked him to report to his suite.

Within minutes his assistant arrived at the door. Rashad invited him inside. Before he backed down from his intentions he said, "I find it necessary for you to assist me with one more matter concerning Mademoiselle Viret. She'll be leaving Al-Shafeeq within the hour." At least that's what he was saying while he still had a shred of princely honor left.

His assistant looked shocked, but said nothing. Rashad could always depend on the other man's discretion even if he'd witnessed his secret comings and goings from the American's room.

"I want you to accompany her to El-Joktor and see that she's put on the flight to Geneva leaving at four this afternoon. The reservation has already been made. I'll bring her to the eastern gate and meet you there in a half hour."

"Very good, Your Highness."

With Nazir gone, Rashad left his quarters for the garden suite. After being out in the heat, he imagined Lauren would be resting with an icy fruit drink. Little did she know she was about to be scuttled away from the palace into a helicopter and flown far away.

Once her jet was in flight, the camel would be out of the tent.

As soon as Lauren had returned to her room, Farah came by for her and asked if she would like to see the new foal her husband had given her?

Lauren grabbed at the invitation. Watching Rafi walk away just now had come close to killing her. She needed company and enjoyed spending time with the princess. After her hope of finding some kind of information on the royal family had had been dashed by the bookshop owner, she could use some cheering up.

During her travels, Lauren had been to great cities and shrines all over the world and had always come away with souvenir books and pamphlets. But as this was her first trip to the Arabian desert, it was possible that under the laws of the Shafeeq dynasty, nothing official was put in print for the public.

She was sorry about that. If she'd been able to purchase such a book, she would have found an expert Arab translator back home to reproduce it in English for her. Naturally there was generic information in encyclopedias and periodicals on some facet of tribal warfare. But she would have treasured a tome on the royal family. After all, she shared a portion of the blood flowing through Farah's veins. Some of their DNA was the same.

While they were exclaiming over the adorable new filly, Farah was called to the phone. She was only gone a brief time. When she returned she said, "That was Nazir. He says you are to go to your suite right away."

A frown marred Lauren's brow. "Why?"

The princess shook her head. "I don't know, but it sounded important. I'll walk you back."

"That won't be necessary, Farah. I know my way now. Thank you for bringing me here. I'll talk to you later."

Maybe he had a private message from Rafi.

Nazir met her outside the door to her suite. "Thank you for coming so quickly, mademoiselle. If I might speak to you?"

"Of course."

She opened the door and went inside. He followed. "I am here to inform you that the king is aware of your distress after being caught in the sandstorm. Since he doesn't want you to have to wait any longer for a caravan, he has given his permission for you to be flown by helicopter to El-Joktor immediately. I will accompany you to your jet which will leave for Geneva at four o'clock this afternoon."

Lauren reeled, incapable of speech. With these plans having been made, it meant she would never see Rafi again. So that was why he'd taken her on a tour of the Oasis this morning. He'd known her time was up. Her heart shriveled at the realization.

"If you will be so kind as to pack, I will ask the staff to take your personal belongings to the helicopter waiting outside the gate. You have time to eat your lunch. It is waiting on the table. Do you have any questions for me? Otherwise I'll return in thirty minutes."

She was so shocked by the turn of events she couldn't think straight. "Wh-what about my passport?" her voice faltered.

"It will be given to you at the airport. Is there anything else?"

"No," she whispered in absolute agony. For once her pain was too deep for tears. "I'll be ready." She despised the tremor in her voice that revealed her emotions.

"Very good, mademoiselle."

The second Nazir left, she ran to her bedroom and packed, realizing it was all over. She would fly away, but her heart would remain here. She wondered what Rafi would say if she told him she didn't want to leave yet.

She wished there were some way she could delay her departure, if only for another day. *He'd* become the most important thing in her life. Lauren wasn't ready to be ripped away from him, but fate had decreed it.

When she carried her suitcases into the sitting room, she saw her lunch tray, but couldn't possibly eat and sank down on a chair to wait.

"Lauren?" Rafi entered the room without knocking.

She looked at him, then glanced away quickly. "Nazir told me the king has arranged for me to leave. I'm glad you came so I could say goodbye to you and thank you for everything."

He came closer. "You look ill."

"I'm sorry if you've caught me reacting to the news."

"You don't wish to leave yet?"

"I'm sure that sounds ludicrous to you."

"Not at all," he said in a benign voice. "You Americans have a saying. 'Better to take the hell you're sure of.' It's only natural to cling to what is real to you here rather than return to an uncertain future without your grandmother."

"Who made you so wise?" She smiled gently at him.

"Perhaps not that wise since I'm not satisfied you're telling me everything. I insist you unburden yourself." He hunkered down and grasped her hands. She loved it when he touched her. Lauren never wanted him to stop.

"Why do you think there's anything more?"

"Because the little nerve in your throat never stops throbbing."

She immediately pulled one of her hands away to cover the spot.

"You see?" he asked silkily. "One can try to hide, but the body will always give something away."

"You think I'm hiding something?"

He turned her hand over and made circles against her palm with his thumb. The sensation was so erotic, he had to have heard her moan. "I know you are," he whispered.

She couldn't take any more. "There is one thing, but it's an entirely selfish wish on my part. I wouldn't want the king to think I was ungrateful for everything he's made possible. I'll always be in his debt, and *yours*, even though you deny much of the part you played in my being well enough to g-go home," her voice broke.

She didn't have a sense of home anymore and Rafi knew it. Maybe she really was ill and would need to see a psychiatrist when she finally returned to Switzerland. "Nazir will be here soon. I think I have everything." She tried to remove her hand and get up, but his rock-hard body blocked any movement.

"Look at me," he said in a husky tone that sounded more like a command.

Lauren did his bidding and found herself wanting to fall into him.

His gaze fell on her lips. She had the sensation of being kissed, yet he'd done nothing! "What's the one thing you want?"

The one thing she wanted was to stay here with him, but she knew that was impossible. Still, if she could have a few more days. He couldn't help but hear the dangerous knock of her heart against her ribs.

"Mustafa mentioned a place called the Garden of the Moon. He said I would especially appreciate it." She'd already lied about their caravan driver once, but the risk of revealing the real reason she wanted to see it was too great.

"Maybe it's foolish of me, but after coming all this way, when I'll never be here again, it seems such a shame not to see it before I leave, but Princess Farah said it's not allowed."

His hands tightened almost painfully on her fingers before letting them go, but she welcomed the pain. It made her feel closer to him. "It's forbidden to tourists, but I'll make an exception for you this one time." His words came out sounding like a vow. He rose to his full, intimidating height and looked down at her with glittering black eyes.

She was thankful to be sitting because after hearing that she'd been given a reprieve, her body caved. "But the arrangements to return to El-Joktor—"

"They can be changed. A few more days will make no difference in the scheme of things. Nazir will take care of everything."

She finally stood up on legs of rubber, staring into his eyes. "You really mean it?"

He cocked his dark head. His male beauty shook her to the core. "You should have said something earlier. It's a small thing you ask."

"No, it's not." She breathed heavily. "Everything you do for me causes an inconvenience to someone, but I appreciate this more than you can imagine."

"I believe you." There was no hint of mockery just then. "Now you have to do a favor for me."

"Anything."

She heard his sharp intake of breath, not realizing she might have sounded as if she were being provocative on purpose. "In order to get the full benefit of the garden, you have to see it after the moon comes up. Therefore, I want you to rest and I hope, get some sleep. I'll come for you tonight at seven-thirty. Eat a filling dinner."

"I will."

"Have you ever ridden a horse?"

"Many times."

Something flickered in the dark recesses of his eyes. "Wear boots and bring your cloak to keep you warm. Today it was hot in the desert, but tonight the temperature will drop."

She smoothed an errant curl off her forehead. "Don't you have to stay at the palace on duty?"

A strange gleam entered his eyes. He studied her for a moment. "Several of my staff are always available."

"But what if it's an emergency and you're needed?"

"I always keep my phone with me. If necessary Nazir would send a helicopter for us."

He started walking toward the door. She followed him. "Then I'm relieved."

"Remember to get plenty of rest."

After his tall, powerful body disappeared out the doors, she walked through the suite to the garden unable to contain her joy. *Rafi*— Tonight they'd be alone together. She leaned over to smell the fragrance of the huge, rare yellow and white hibiscus. Just one night with him. If it was all he was willing to give her, then she'd take it and be grateful.

She folded her arms and clutched them to her waist. This man had a power over her so complete she knew she would die if she couldn't be with him tonight. Anyone hearing that thought expressed would tell her she needed some serious therapy. Anyone except her grandmother who'd made a prediction about her a long time ago.

CHAPTER SIX

RASHAD watched the great orange-red ball sink below the horizon. It wouldn't take long for there to be a drop in temperature that would continue to fall. Night descended fast in the desert. He had no concern. This had been his playground as a boy. He knew all of it. Should the unimaginable happen, such as another sandstorm, the GPS transponder he wore on his wrist would bring help.

He had no idea why Lauren wanted to visit the Garden of the Moon, but before the night was over, he would have his answer. She'd been quiet during their journey from the palace. Too quiet.

He looked back. Her white cloak flapped behind her as the wind blew here and there, tousling her blond curls. She rode as though she'd been born on a horse and allowed her mare, Zia, to follow behind his stallion. Smart woman, smart horse.

Zia was a product of the desert and had learned early to plant her hooves where Jabbar had already displaced the sand. That way she preserved her strength. Both horses had been packed with everything Rashad required for them to spend the night together.

His gorgeous tent intruder was out to seduce him in earnest. When he'd found her waiting in the sitting room, seduction had been on her mind. Unshed tears of a devil or an angel. It made little difference at this point.

Because she desired him on top of the mission she had yet to carry out, he was looking forward to the experience more than anything he'd anticipated in his life. Tonight there'd be a three-quarter moon. By the time they reached their destination and made camp, the lesser light would appear in the black canopy enveloping them.

Halfway there Rashad pulled back on the reins to allow Lauren time to come alongside him. He darted her a searching glance. Heat rising from the sand wafted before their faces. "Would you like to rest?"

"If you're worried I'm tired, I'm not. But if you want to stop for a minute, that's fine."

"I think I do." He reached for his water bag and drank his fill. She followed suit with her own.

Rashad had made camp hundreds, maybe thousands of times in his life, but never with a woman because he and his men always had to be on their guard. Having her along was an entirely new experience, and it raised the stakes.

As she lowered her bag, their eyes met. He could no longer see the color in hers, but the luminescence still shone through in the darkness. An enchantress. That's what she was.

Eager to make camp, he tucked in his water bag and rode on without saying anything to her. She caught up to him again and stayed at his side. From time to time he gave her covert glances. To his continual amazement she looked around with an air of suppressed excitement. She seemed too happy. Nothing had ever twisted his insides like this before.

"We're almost there. After we ride this long dune to the top, we will have arrived."

"I can't wait—" she cried, then raced up the slope ahead of him. She rode hard. The sight of her cloak flying behind her was like poetry in motion. Poor Zia had to be in shock.

None of his bodyguards had sounded an alarm. Clearly there were was no one out here tonight except the two of them. On a burst of exhilaration because he had another twelve hours alone with her, Rashad charged after her, bursting the bonds that had held him back.

Just once she looked behind her. When she saw him gaining on her, she laughed and urged Zia on. He overtook her before she reached the top. Feeling like a schoolboy, he leaped from the saddle.

While he waited for her to appear, he drew two parts of one of his tent poles from the camping gear and connected them. Once he'd buried the end of it in the sand, he tethered his horse's reins to it.

In another minute she came riding up the crest. He walked toward her and reached for Zia's bit to slow her down.

"That was wonderful!"

She dismounted without his help, sounding winded and carefree. If he hadn't held her sobbing body in his arms several times, he wouldn't know this laughing, happy woman was the same person. "What can I do to help?"

Rashad smiled as he led Zia to the pole to attach her reins. "We'll unload the horses and put up our tent first."

He'd purposely said *our* tent, not surprised he didn't meet with any modest protest. They worked in harmony to get it erected. She exclaimed over the beautiful rug he'd brought to put on the floor of their small tent. More sounds of excitement poured out of her as he layered the rug with silk duvets and pillows.

"Those are going to feel good. You were right.

It's already getting chilly." While they were watering the horses she said, "Are we going to make a fire?"

"No. It would spoil the effect."

"What effect?"

"Moonlight. The essential ingredient to bring the garden to life. Didn't Mustafa tell you?"

"No," came her subdued response.

But someone else had.

"In the beginning, our tribe worshipped the moon god because they were a pastoral people who kept watch over their flocks at night. This garden you're going to see represents the moon god's abode. It's a sacred place and ancient as time itself. The nearby oasis is the moon god's gift to the tribe to make sure there's an abundance of water to keep it green year-round. The palace was built there for that reason."

"What a fascinating story. Thank you for enlightening me."

For a long time she'd been playing her game with the expertise of a master, but once she saw the garden, he would bring it to an end. In a lithe movement he pulled a little pouch out of his saddlebag and handed it to her. "Here. Have some *qandi*."

"What is that?"

"Candy. You Americans borrowed the word."

He felt her smile as she dipped her hand inside and withdraw some sugar-coated almonds. "Um. These are delicious." She took a few and gave him back the bag. He tossed several in his mouth before putting it inside the opening of the tent.

Rashad glanced up at the eastern sky. While they'd been busy, the moon had been making her ascent. It was time. "Walk with me up to the curl of the dune." He reached for her hand. As their fingers entwined, he felt that same quickening in his blood, but it was much stronger than on the day of the sandstorm.

With each step of their short trek, he realized he'd been tempting fate all along. It was far too late to turn back now. He didn't want to. In fact no power could make him. That was the terrifying part.

* * *

Lauren's grandmother had told her that the sheikh had taken her to the Garden of the Moon, but she'd only talked to her about Malik and what had happened with him, not about the garden itself.

When they reached the edge and Lauren looked down, she could never have conceived of the sight that met her eyes. The man at her side squeezed her hand tighter, conveying emotion she thought she understood, but still waters ran deep inside him.

A drastic change had occurred in the landscape. The dune served as an escarpment. Below she saw fantastic formations laid out so perfectly, she let out a cry of astonishment. They looked like huge, fat topiary trees, the kind you see in the parterre gardens of the Orangerie at Versailles in France. Only they were made of sand sculpted by strange wind currents favoring this particular area of the dunes.

She was so staggered, it took her a long time to take it all in. Finally she exhaled a breath.

'This is the most extraordinary, beautiful, out-of-this-world sight I'll ever see in my lifetime. No wonder your tribe has always held this spot sacred. So do I," she whispered.

It explained the half moon on the medallion King Malik had given her grandmother. Everything made sense. Her hand went automatically to her throat to feel it, forgetting it was no longer there. The same wind that had torn it off her had carved this monument. There were forces here she didn't understand. Hairs lifted on her arms that had nothing to do with the chill of the night.

"Cold?" he inquired in a quiet voice, never letting go of her hand.

She was running hot and cold at the same time. "Yes."

"It's late. You go back to the tent. I'll join you in a minute."

Her pulse quickened as she started back. Already the wind, dancing about, had erased the footprints they'd made coming up. *It is written in the wind* was a phrase she'd heard many times. Now she understood what it meant.

The wind had changed her life. She wasn't the same woman who'd flown to El-Joktor on a quest to know more about her grandfather. That woman had been buried in the sand. After her body had been transported to Al-Shafeeq, a new woman had been brought back to life by forces greater than she knew, by a man greater than any other.

Taking advantage of being alone, she lifted the tent flap and tossed her cloak inside, then went around the back. When she'd refreshed herself, she moved to the front and sat down inside the doorway to pull off her boots. After she'd held them over the sand and tipped them upside down, she emptied her socks and stashed everything in a corner with her cloak.

The wind blew enough that she lowered the flap to keep out the sand. It was pitch-dark inside, but she loved it. Still in her jeans and cotton top, she picked her side and climbed under one of the puffy quilts. Tucking the nearest pillow beneath her head, she lay there and waited while he did whatever needed doing to make their camp secure.

Soon she saw a small glow and watched his shadow as he moved about. After a few minutes the flap went up. He'd lit a lantern beneath an overhang with sides that prevented the wind from coming in. He set it on a rug he'd rolled out. Next to it sat a bowl of water and a pile of hand towels. He'd already removed his cloak and boots.

Her gaze flew to his in surprise. The black fires in his eyes started her body trembling. She lay there entranced. "Are you thirsty?"

"A little."

He handed her the water bag. After she'd drunk from it, he put his mouth to the same place and drank. The gesture wasn't wasted on her. She watched the way the cords worked in his throat. His male beauty captivated her.

"Hand me your boots. I'll put them with mine." She did his bidding. "Now stretch your hands toward me."

She got to her knees and put out her hands. He
knelt before her and dipped a towel in the water
before washing them. The water was warm and
scented with the faint fragrance of rose.

No one had ever washed her hands for her
before. When he reached for another towel, she
got a fluttery feeling in her chest. This time he
began washing her face. With slow gentle strokes
he covered her forehead and cheeks, her nose and
mouth. With the tenderest of touches he wiped
her neck and throat, even her ears.

Once he put the towel aside, she took a clear
one. Imitating his actions, she washed his hands
and forearms, wanting to bring him the same
exquisite pleasure. His body was a miracle to her.
She relished being able to touch him like this.

Another dip in the water and she was able to
bathe his face to her heart's content, from his
widow's peak to the crease in his bold chin. He'd
shaved before coming. She marveled over his
incredible olive skin burnished by the elements.
His black eyebrows were beautifully shaped. His

nose—every bold, rugged feature—was perfect to her.

Then there was his mouth. Like the mesmerizing dunes, its shape changed with his mood. Hard, soft, brooding, compelling. *Sensuous.* She put the towel aside, needing to feel it beneath hers. She ran her thumb across it, aching with need.

"Oh, Rafi," her voice shook. "If you don't kiss me again, I think I'm going to die."

"I've already died several deaths because of you," he whispered against her lips. "What a perfect mouth you have. I came close to eating you alive at the cabaret. That's why I forced us to leave. I didn't trust myself."

He cupped her face in his hands and began with a series of light kisses he pressed to all the places he'd washed, barely grazing her mouth.

She wasn't satisfied and protested with a moan. "Don't tease me. I can't take it."

"Then show me what you want," he said in a voice of velvet.

"You *know* what I want. *This*." She wrapped her arms around his neck and covered his mouth with her own, not allowing him any hiding place. A profound hunger had grown inside her. She was after his soul and his mouth was the conduit.

"Lauren—" he cried her name. His hands roamed her back and waist, drawing her into him as they drank both deeper and deeper. Her passion for him was so intense, her body quivered.

He lay her back down and followed her, giving her the kiss she'd been dying for. He was starving for her, too. She knew he was, but after a few minutes she seemed to be doing most of the work.

While the cold wind blew against the tent, a fire roared inside her. Her body, her senses yearned for him. Every kiss had grown more intoxicating, yet she felt he was still holding back and couldn't understand it. Was something wrong?

"I want you, Rafi, and know you want me. I want you to love me all night," she cried from the depths of her being. "What's stopping you? Have I grown less desirable?"

"No." He sounded so distant. How could that be when only a little while ago he'd washed her hands and face in a ceremony so erotic, she would never be the same again. "You're infinitely desirable and you know it."

"Then—"

"Tell me who you are, Lauren Viret," he broke in.

"Who *am* I?" she whispered dazedly. She didn't understand. "What do you mean?"

"The Garden of the Moon is a sacred place of the royal family no one knows about, yet you admit you had knowledge of it before you came here. You claim that it was Mustafa who informed you. But if that's really true, then he will have to be punished."

"What?" Her intoxication had been so complete, she could scarcely comprehend he'd brought an end to their rapture. She sat up to clear her head.

"Mustafa knows there's a penalty for divulging that information."

"No—" she cried out, putting her hands on his arm. "He wasn't the person who told me. I swear it! He's a good man who saved me from the storm."

Rashad raised up on one elbow. That mouth she loved had tightened to a thin line. She felt his body go rigid beneath her fingers. "Who then?"

He was deadly serious, sending her into shock. "Someone else told me about it."

"Was it Prince Faisal?"

At the mention of the name, she drew in a surprised breath.

"You *do* know him—" Suddenly Rafi sat up and became the forbidding chief of security.

"No—" she cried, shaking her head.

His hands circled her arms. "Don't lie to me, Lauren."

She could hardly swallow. "I'm not, but I did recognize the name just now. Paul, the man who wanted to marry me, told me he'd met a minor

rince from the northern Arabian kingdom at
he casino in Montreux. He'd said his name was
Faisal."

"When was this?"

"A month ago, maybe less. He got an interview
with him and some pictures."

"Go on."

Lauren moistened her lips nervously. "There
isn't much to tell except that he told Paul there
were photographic opportunities in the Nafud
where he would rule supreme one day. When
Paul came back to the apartment, he begged to
come with me to the desert, but I'd already told
him no. Why did you bring up his name to me?"

Lines bracketed Rafi's mouth. "He's the son of
King Umar's brother, a man out to cause trouble
within the Shafeeq family. It's no secret he in-
tends to become king when King Umar dies."

"But King Umar has a son! Princess Farah said
he would be king some day."

"Yes. But that won't stop Faisal from staging a
coup." Rafi let go of her arms. "He's waiting for

news of the king's illness and how close he is to death, but his informers can't get into the palace. Since you refuse to tell me the name of the person who told you about the Garden of the Moon, I made an assumption that there was a connection between you and Faisal. Only a handful of people know about the Garden of the Moon."

"You think I'm a *spy?*"

His eyes glittered dangerously. "Given the facts, what am I supposed to think?"

She couldn't believe this conversation was taking place. "The person who told me about the garden is dead now."

"If you're not working for Faisal, then what's the real reason you've come to Al-Shafeeq?"

"I've already told you," she said in a low voice.

"Yes, but how do I know you were telling me the truth?"

Lauren moaned. *Don't ask me any more questions.* She knew he was only doing his duty for King Umar, but it hurt her so badly she didn't want to talk anymore. He was torturing her. "Why don't you answer me?"

"With your intelligence-gathering team, it would be a simple matter to find out." She was getting in too deep and wanted to howl because it seemed her night of ecstasy wasn't going to happen.

"You lied about Mustafa. Why?"

Help. "To protect someone." *Me. My grand-father. The royal family.*

"You refuse to tell me who it is?"

"I *can't* tell you," she cried in anguish. "Have you never made a promise to someone you swore to keep to the death?"

He examined her upturned face, searching for any sign of weakness. After a tension-filled silence he said, "One."

"So have I, Rafi. One promise in the whole of my life. I can't break it, not even for you."

"Why?"

"Because it could hurt certain people." She drew in a fortifying breath before removing her hands to hug her upraised knees. "Believing that I have lied to you all along, why did you bring me here?"

"To uncover your secret." His voice sounded like the lash of a whip.

"I see." Her heart almost failed her. "Thank you for being honest with me. I thought you wanted to make love to me."

"I do."

"I wanted it, too," her voice throbbed, "more than anything you could imagine. But this thing is between us now. I can't get past it."

"You lived with it before I asked for the truth," he reminded her. That tone of mockery was back.

"I know this won't help, but I'm going to say it anyway. The person who told me about the garden didn't know this place was sacred. Now that you've explained, I'll make you a promise. No one will ever hear about it from me. When I fly away from Al-Shafeeq, the desert wind will sweep all memories from my mind."

She moved away from him and pulled the quilt

over her. Beyond tears, she clutched the pillow, praying for sleep to come and bring this bitter-sweet night to a close.

Outside the tent she heard movement. She could have sworn he said something to the horses, then the light went out. While she lay there holding herself taut, he got in beside her, rustling her covers. He reached over and rolled her into him.

"After being outside, I need your warmth." His mouth descended once more. It was a kiss hot with desire.

Her body quivered before she tore her lips from his and buried her face against his throat. "It's too late. I'm a liar. You hate me for it."

"I would love to hate you," his voice grated, running his hands through her blond silk curls. He wrapped his arms around her. "Your body gives off heat like a furnace. Lucky is the man who warms himself next to you. I'm looking forward to holding you all night."

Being in his arms like this was divine torture.

"I'm not going to ask about the women in your life because we've already had that discussion."

"You have an excellent memory." She felt his lips kiss her hair and brows. "What will you do when you're back in Geneva?"

"I'm not sure." The idea of going to America and starting a new life sounded absurd now. In fact, the thought of leaving this tent was anathema to her.

"Have you no relatives to go to?"

"No. My parents died six months after I was born." *Ask me to stay, Rafi, and I will.* "But I have friends and plenty of money from my grandmother."

"Tell me how she came by her money."

"She was a Melrose from New York. They were in the manufacturing business and they made a fortune before they sold the company, granting my grandmother an income for life. Did I tell you she was a fabulous horsewoman?"

"She taught you well. You ride like one of my countrymen."

"I believe you just paid me a compliment." She would always cherish it. "In New York, we rode all the time and traveled everywhere together. She willed me everything including the apartment in Montreux."

"Why Switzerland?"

"Because it's so beautiful. Have you ever been here?"

"Yes."

"If I'd known you sooner, I would have invited you to the apartment. I can tell you're a horse lover. My grandmother would have loved talking horses with you."

His hands stopped roving over her back. "How do you know about my love of them?"

"I see the special way you care for them. A little while ago I heard you talking to them outside. There's a bond some people have with their horses. My mother had that same bond. She and my grandmother were very close. Now they're all buried next to each other in Montreux."

"That's where your roots are."

Some of them.

"I was born in New York, but we left for Switzerland when I was a child. I suppose that when I go back, I'll finish working on Richard Bancroft's journals. One day they'll be ready for the publisher."

"The way you refer to him, I take it Richard wasn't your grandfather."

She swallowed hard. "No."

"Then who was your mother's father?"

"That was my grandmother's secret." Like grandmother, like granddaughter. "Celia came from a time when you didn't talk about certain things." Lauren had already told him much more than she should have. "Goodnight, Rafi."

When she tried to turn away, he kept her held against him and locked his legs around hers. She was so on fire for him, she was afraid she'd stay awake the rest of the night. But she hadn't counted on how wonderful it was to lie in his arms where she could feel his heart pounding against hers. He was a bastion of safety. The sense of being protected came as a revelation. She nestled closer to him and knew nothing more until the smell of coffee brought her awake.

Lauren sat up with a start because Rafi wasn't still holding her. Outside the tent, the sky was blue. Inside was warm. She didn't need her covers. No telling how long the sun had been up.

"Rafi?" She hurriedly reached for her socks and boots and put them on. He'd already been doing housekeeping chores. She wanted to help.

"Good morning, Lauren," he said in a voice an octave deeper than usual. His penetrating black gaze took in her complete disarray. He on the other hand looked magnificent as always. "Sleep well?"

The wind had died down. She pushed the errant curls out of her face. "What do *you* think?"

His lips twitched. When they did that, she almost had a coronary. "I think you should sleep with a man more often." But Rafi didn't mean himself. This was his goodbye speech and it hurt so terribly she wanted to cry it to the desert surrounding them. "Nine hours has done you a world of good."

"Nine? I slept that long? When did *you* wake up?"

"Half an hour ago." He handed her a mug of coffee he'd heated on a little burner.

She took a few sips. "Ambrosia. My compliments to the chef." She looked around and decided to walk up to the edge of dune, but Rafi stopped her.

"Don't."

Lauren turned to face him. "Why?"

"Let the picture of last night be the one to fill your mind when you leave for El-Joktor tomorrow morning. Without the moonlight, its impact is lost."

Tomorrow morning?

Pain caused her to take a deep breath. "I'm sure you're right."

"Try this." He handed her a roll from one of the bags. "It's sweet and will take the edge off your appetite until we return to the palace."

"Do we have to get right back?" Then she shook her head. "Wait—don't answer that. Duty calls and I've taken up too much of your time." She finished her food before returning to the tent to roll up the quilts and carry everything out to the horses for Rafi.

He was in a mood she couldn't decipher. Lauren knew that in his mind she had lied to him and continued to do so, but she felt no hostility from him. She sensed he had worries on his mind that had nothing to do with her.

Life without Rafi. *It is what it is, Lauren.*

Unlike her grandmother so many years ago, she wouldn't be going home pregnant with her lover's child. How much she suddenly longed to leave pregnant with Rafi's baby. He would never know and she could never tell him.

She worked faster to stave off her pain. Without his asking, she helped him dismantle the tent. Once the stakes and poles were packed, they were ready to leave. She threw on her cloak and headscarf before mounting Zia, but inside she was groaning from unbearable heartache.

He approached her side on his stallion and flicked her a glance. Their eyes clung for a moment. "Ready?" She nodded. They started out, making faster progress than they had last night. The horses knew where they were going. Zia was happy to have free rein.

Lauren purposely fell behind Rafi so she could feast her eyes on him in his robe and headdress for as long as possible. This episode in her life was fast coming to an end. She didn't want to miss a second of it.

Every so often they stopped to drink from their water bags, then pushed on without talking. They'd said it all last night in the tent. Rafi wanted to hate her for lying to him. She could never get past that with him.

Before long they came in sight of the Oasis. Lauren had once read that a Bedouin burst into poetry and song when he saw the greenness after being many weeks in the sand-drenched wilderness. She'd thought it such an odd thing to do until she too had been out in it.

Ah, Rafi... I can't bear to lose you.

The palace loomed ahead. They made their way to the west entrance where Nazir and two other staff were waiting for them.

"I'll contact you later." As Rafi dismounted, she scanned his face, which had been scarfed the whole time except for his eyes. With the bearing of a prince, he walked away from her and disappeared. Naturally his first priority was to report for work, but she almost begged him not to leave her.

Needing an outlet for her emotions, she leaned forward to pat Zia, then dismounted quickly.

"Welcome back, mademoiselle. A hot bath and a meal are awaiting you."

"Thank you, Nazir." While he escorted her inside, the two other men took care of the horses.

He left her outside the door of her suite and she hurried inside. After removing her cloak and boots, she quickly discarded her clothes and

stepped into the bath. Rafi had ordered it especially for her because he knew how good it would
feel after riding beneath a blistering sun.

But wonderful as the scented water felt lapping
around her head and body, she'd sell her soul for
another night like last night. She closed her eyes,
replaying every second from the moment he'd
started washing her hands with the towel.

He'd created a world of beauty for her inside
that tent. They were the acts of a man who worshipped the woman he loved. If there were no
lies to have destroyed his trust, would he have
worshipped her enough to ask her to stay here
at Al-Shafeeq because he couldn't live without
her?

She knew what her answer would be, but realized the question would never pass his lips.

After his shower, Rashad hitched a towel around
his hips and drank a cup of black coffee. He'd
had his sources checking on facts for him since

early morning. So far everything Lauren had told him was the truth.

There had indeed been a Melrose family from New York that had made a fortune in manufacturing. Certain other facts had also been verified. As for Mustafa, she'd even admitted lying about him in order to protect him because she didn't want the poor man punished. She'd convinced him Faisal hadn't been involved, too.

He tossed the medallion and chain in his palm. The gold he held in his hand proved she'd come to Al-Shafeeq on a mission she still refused to talk about. But even not knowing the reason hadn't mattered to him last night. He'd wanted to make love to her and would have, but for the one thing his father had engrained in him from the time he'd come of age.

"You're a prince, destined to be king, Rashad. Enjoy our women at your discretion, but stay away from forbidden fruit. The strongest man can be tempted to take a bite. Once he does, he will eat the whole and lose his way because of it.

"*You,* my son, don't have that luxury. For that to happen to you will bring disappointment to your mother and me, but that is nothing compared to the shame and dishonor you will bring upon yourself. You cannot reclaim your honor once it is gone, therefore you cannot be an honorable husband and father to your children, let alone serve a nation that needs its strongest son to rule.'

When Rashad would have lost his head at the last moment, a picture of his wedding night to an innocent Princess Azzah in a month's time wouldn't let go of him and cooled his blood.

Tomorrow morning Nazir would accompany Lauren to El-Joktor. *As he should have done yesterday,* but for Rashad's need of her. It was so great, he'd gone off with her instead. Now his agony was at its zenith.

Today he would fly to Raz and immerse himself in work. He might even stay over in order to avoid further temptation and not return to the palace until tomorrow after she'd gone. It was a lame plan, but he was a desperate man.

Even if he pressured her enough to know the whole truth, it would change nothing. His life's path had been set from the moment he was born. She was the forbidden fruit. The ultimate test. He checked his watch. Twenty hours from now, she'd be gone. *Forever.* That word was so hideous, he couldn't dress or get away from the palace fast enough.

Once he reached Raz, he drove the Jeep to the outskirts where the foundation of the new refinery would be built. After levering himself from the seat, he walked around the perimeter, wanting to get a feel for it before the actual work began.

His plan for a new era of prosperity was about to get underway. In time they'd make enough money to build more infrastructure. The list of things to be done stretched from one end of the kingdom to the other.

He looked all around, brushing the sweat off his brows with his forearm. On the one hand,

Rashad had been blessed in abundance. On the other, he was denied the one thing that brough a man true happiness.

According to his father, Rashad couldn't have that. He was a prince, and that kind of happiness was for ordinary men like Tariq. His assistan couldn't wait to go home every night to his bec where he found the woman he loved waiting for him.

Rashad's father had been right about one thing He'd tasted Lauren last night and her fruit had been so sweet, he knew he would crave it over and over again for the rest of his life. That was his penance.

How many years was he going to be tortured by her taste? One misstep had already eaten away at his soul. His eyes smarted.

He supposed if there was one mercy, it was that Princess Azzah would have no expectations Undoubtedly she too had a secret love she would have to say goodbye to in order to obey her own father. Rashad could conceive of no greater hel

han to sleep with her when both of them would
only be going through the motions in order to
produce offspring.

His father had done it. So had his mother. So
had his grandparents. Somehow they'd all lived
through it and survived.

In the end, was that all it meant? To survive?

His thoughts were so dark and grim, Tariq had
to remind him his phone was ringing. He glanced
at the caller ID. Why would Farah be phoning
him? If it wasn't about their father, then this had
to do with Lauren. He felt a rush of adrenaline
before he clicked on.

"Farah?"

"Forgive me for disturbing you. Can you talk?"

"Yes." He walked a little distance off where the
others couldn't hear him. "Is this about Father?"

"No. It's about Lauren."

His body tautened. "Go on."

"I don't quite know how to say this."

He shifted his weight. "Just come to the point."

"Lauren isn't like the other women you've enjoyed over the years, Rafi. I'm afraid she has taken your attention too seriously."

His hand formed a fist. "Why do you say that?"

"Because I've been with her this afternoon. She told me she's leaving tomorrow, but she shows all the signs of a woman who doesn't want to go."

Tell me something I don't already know, Farah. The thought of Lauren never coming back was destroying him.

"You're usually so careful. I think she's really hurting."

"What would you have me do?"

"I don't know. Talk to Father. Tell him you're not ready to get married and see where this thing leads with you and Lauren. I like her very much."

"It can't lead anywhere. You know that."

"No, I *don't* know that! You'll be king one day. Prevail on father to change the rules. A good king is a better king if he's happy!"

His throat swelled because Farah was his champion. "You want me to change centuries of tradition to take what I want?"

"Yes—if it means you can live your life with the woman you love."

"I never said I loved her."

"You didn't have to. You're a different man since you flew her out of the sandstorm. There's a look in your eyes I've never seen before. Our sisters have noticed, too. If you let her go, then you have a stone for a heart. When father's gone, you won't have to worry about filling his shoes. Yours will crush his." She rang off.

The silence on the other end deafened him. He spun around and raced back to his Jeep. Tariq joined him in the front seat. "What's wrong, Your Highness?"

"You don't want to know. I have to get back to the palace immediately."

En route he phoned Nazir and told him to keep an eye on Lauren's activities. Nazir was able to tell him she was having dinner in Princess Farah's suite. Rashad gave him further instructions about the plans for her flight to El-Joktor in the morning, then he hung up.

Once he arrived at the palace, he went to his suite for a shower and change of clothes. He decided to wear a suit in a stone-gray color with a white shirt and tie. After a visit to his office to clean up some paperwork, he left for the garden suite with the half dozen newspapers he hadn't read that morning.

Normally he scanned them before leaving for Raz. He didn't trust the television to tell the truth about anything. The printed news wasn't much better, but there were a few editorials that informed to a certain extent.

He let himself inside Lauren's suite and turned on the lamp at the desk after ordering his dinner and a carafe of hot coffee. While he waited for it to arrive, he made a call to his mechanic to be sure everything would be ready for tomorrow's flight.

Once he was served his food, he sat down and began reading. By the time he'd gotten to the fourth newspaper, he heard the door open and looked up.

The blonde woman who entered the sitting room wore the sleeveless black dress from her luggage and a pair of black high heels. Between her stunning face and figure, his lungs tightened in reaction.

She stopped in her tracks when she saw him. "Rafi— I didn't realize you were in here or I would have left Farah's suite sooner."

"I only got back from Raz a little while ago." He put down the paper. "In another minute I would have come looking for you. How was your dinner with Princess Farah?"

"We had a lovely time."

"What did you do?"

She stood there, rather nervously, he thought. "Mostly she talked about her brother. Their thirty-fifth birthday is coming up and she's in charge of getting the present for him while her sisters plan the party. We discussed everything from horse blankets and saddles, to a bronze of some kind for his desk. She still hasn't made up her mind."

He nodded and got to his feet. "And what did *you* talk about?"

"This and that." She rubbed her arms. "Look—I've imposed so much on your time I feel guilty. You don't have to keep me company. I need a good night's sleep before I leave in the morning. Why don't we just say goodbye now."

"You *want* to say goodnight?"

CHAPTER SEVEN

LAUREN averted her eyes. "I think it would be best. I have to pack." She started for the bedroom, but Rafi followed her. With her heart thudding, she stepped out of her high heels and walked over to the wardrobe to get her suitcases.

After putting them on the bed, she packed her boots and high heels followed by her cloak and headscarf. Then she emptied the drawers. The pants and blouse she planned to wear on the flight home she laid out on the back of the dressing-table chair with her sandals. It didn't take her long to get the bulk of it done.

He stayed where he was with his hands at his sides. She noticed they were forming fists. Good. She was glad to see he wasn't in control any more than she was. Had he decided he wanted to make

love to her after all? Maybe she'd make it easy
for him.

Without glancing in his direction, she unzipped
her dress and stepped out of it, putting it on top.
After shutting the cases, she set them on the
floor. Beneath her dress she wore a modest slip
over her underwear. It covered her better than
the cotton shift from the hospital had done.

When he did nothing, she looked at him half
in longing, half in despair. "What is it you want
Rafi?"

He moved closer. His black eyes raked her body
"I'm going to ask this one more time. Tell me
why you came to the Oasis and why you wanted
to see the Garden of the Moon. Then we'll really
talk."

"I'm sorry, but I told you I made a promise to
someone and that's why I can't tell you." Ignoring
him, she turned off the light and got into bed
pulling the covers over her. "Goodnight. I'll be
ready in the morning when Nazir comes for me.'

Suddenly he flung his suit jacket and tie on

the end of the bed. The next thing she knew he'd pulled up a chair and sat next to her like he'd done that first day. "Don't you know there are factions that would cause harm to the king and his family?"

"I realize that," she came back. "But I'm not one of them. If you recall, I wanted to leave the palace and return to El-Joktor as soon as I was able to stand on my own two feet without fainting. You've had the authority to send me on my way at any given moment."

He nodded his dark head. "That's true, but there was a reason why I didn't, and you know what it is," his voice rasped.

"You mean because of our attraction to each other."

"What else?" Rafi reached for her hand. She tried to pull away, but he was too strong and clasped it. "You can tell me the truth. I'll keep your secret. I swear an oath on it."

Her lower lip trembled. "I swore an oath, too."

She heard him breathe heavily. "Then we're deadlocked."

"I guess we are."

"This isn't the way it has to be." He looked forbidding in the semi-darkness.

"It isn't the way I want it to be either." Whether he knew it or not, he was rubbing his thumb across her palm, sending little darts of aware- ness through her body. This was agony in a new dimension. "Please let go of me." If he went on touching her, she'd beg him to spend the night with her.

He released her hand as though it were a hot potato and shot to his feet. "Is there no reasoning with you?" he asked in a harsh whisper. "No way to reach you on any level?" She'd never heard him angry before.

"Not any more than there was a way for me to reach you last night, even when I threw myself at you. Your seduction of me was complete. I've been reduced to nothing. You can consider me your greatest triumph. You and I have reached the bitter end. Do what you have to do to me."

She couldn't bear it when she saw him get up and reach for his jacket and tie. It meant he was leaving, and this time he wouldn't be back. He was almost to the door.

"Rafi?" she cried out. "There's *one* confession I will make."

He wheeled around, his body alert.

"I want you to know that you made me *live* and *feel* like I've never lived and felt before. That's a distinction no other man will ever hold."

Lauren lost track of time before he left the room. It hurt so much to think he suspected her of some wrongdoing, she'd taken off her dress to provoke him to action. Never in her life had she done anything so outrageous. No one who'd known her before she'd come to the desert would recognize the person she'd become. She didn't know herself anymore.

What was really insane was that a part of her

wished he would detain her here forever. Tha
way she wouldn't be separated from him.

Of course, in her heart of hearts he wouldn't d
such a thing because he wasn't that kind of man
But he *would* send her away in the morning.

Knowing she wouldn't be able to sleep for a
long time, she walked out to the patio to breathe
in the scent of the flowers. She marveled tha
they grew and thrived in one of the harshest o
climates on earth.

Lauren moved around to look at each one and
savor its fragrance. He'd brought her out here the
first time they'd eaten together. The night had
been magical.

Tonight was different. It was late and the air
had grown cooler. One glance at the desert and
she finally went back to the bedroom, hoping
she'd be able to sleep. But her thoughts were too
full of him and it was hours before oblivion took
over.

When morning came, a numbness seemed
to have taken over her body. Once she'd eaten

breakfast, Nazir arrived for her. Before that, several maids had taken her bags on ahead. Nazir escorted her out of the palace to the waiting helicopter. Naturally there was no sign of Rafi. It almost destroyed her, but there was nothing she could do about that now.

She climbed in the back seat next to one of the guards and strapped herself in, having to accept her fate. Nazir took the co-pilot's seat. After he'd put on his head gear they were off. Lauren couldn't bring herself to look back. Frozen with pain, she closed her eyes.

"Mademoiselle? Do you feel ill?"

Nazir always did his job. He would report everything that went on to Rafi. If nothing else, her pride couldn't bear for him to be told she'd had a meltdown in the helicopter on the way to El-Joktor, so she opened her eyes and smiled. "I'm fine. Just sleepy."

He nodded, but he clearly didn't believe her. A heavy sigh escaped her throat.

For once there were clouds in the sky. Not serious ones. They were too high and wispy. The Nafud only got a little more than an inch of rain in a whole year. There'd be no storm today.

She heard the pilot talking through his headphone, most likely to the control tower in El-Joktor. The forty miles that would have taken two days to cover by caravan would only take fifteen minutes or less. They'd already been in the air for a while.

The next time she looked out the window, she saw they were making their approach, but as they drew closer, she realized it was to a smaller city than El-Joktor with a ridge of mountains behind it. Houses, horses, trucks, cars, Jeeps.

"Nazir? What city is this?"

"Raz, mademoiselle."

"Why are we landing here? Is something wrong?"

"No, mademoiselle. Don't be concerned. You're perfectly safe."

The pilot put the helicopter down next to a

sprawling one-story building at what looked like a mining site.

"If you'll follow me," Nazir said after she'd jumped to the ground. He was so polite when he knew he'd left her with no choice. He led her inside the modern, air-conditioned interior. It was a well-decorated office building with every convenience.

"This way, mademoiselle." He showed her around one corner and opened a door for her to step inside. It was a CEO's suite, to be sure. "Please be seated." She sat down on one of the leather chairs. Nazir disappeared, then came back with a bottle of cold water and handed it to her.

"Thank you."

"You're welcome. If you need a restroom, it's through that door."

Once he'd gone, she removed the bottle cap and drank while she awaited her fate. When Rafi walked in through a connecting door, the bottle slipped from her hand and fell to the floor. What little liquid was left spilled on the rug.

He retrieved it before she could, and set it on the desk. "Don't worry. It will dry soon enough." She stared up at him. "This is where I spend the majority of my time."

He'd dressed in typical Arab garb, white top and white pants. He'd tucked them into his leather boots. Rafi was all male; whatever he wore, he looked spectacular.

"Your job covers a lot of territory. It makes a woman's head spin. Why didn't you let the helicopter fly me to El-Joktor?"

His eyes smoldered, sending another delicious shiver down her spine. "Because there's a matter of unfinished business."

"I was afraid of that." She had the pleasure of watching the muscles harden in his striking face.

"Close your eyes and lower your head, Lauren."

If this was some kind of a test, she was determined to meet it with a brave face. "They're closed."

Even before his hands encircled her neck, her heart had jumped to her throat. She felt his legs press against hers while he fastened something at her nape. After he stepped back he said, "You can open them now."

As she lifted her head, she felt something dangling against her chest. She looked down, not believing her eyes. *"My medallion!"* Her gaze flew to his. She discovered him lounging against his desk with a strange gleam in his eyes.

He nodded. "The second Dr. Tamam saw it, he took it off the chain and informed me. While you were still unconscious, I removed the chain from your neck and pocketed both for safekeeping."

Lauren could hardly breathe. "All this time you've had it, yet you flew me to the site of the sandstorm in my pathetic hope to find it?" She covered her mouth with her hand. "Since I was brought in, you've known everything!"

"Not quite." He folded his arms.

"Until the other night, I didn't realize the ancients of your tribe worshipped the moon. The medallion had much more significance than I'd realized." She shook her head.

"I'd hoped you'd tell me the whole story behind it so I wouldn't have to resort to these extreme measures. This is your last chance to come clean. Why didn't you give me the complete description of the medallion when I asked you?"

She unconsciously ran her thumb over the relief. "Because I needed to protect certain people from being hurt in case they saw it and made a connection."

"Certain people at the Oasis, you mean."

Lauren looked away. "Yes."

"And what connection would that be?"

"I thought you knew—" she cried out, jumping to her feet.

"I do, but I want to hear you say it."

There was no help for it. "To the royal family."

"Be more specific."

It was no use. Lauren couldn't take any more. "Oh, all right! To King Malik."

He straightened from the desk. "Why single out King Malik? The medallion is the symbol of

he entire royal family who've been in power for
centuries."

"Because *he* was the one who gave it to…some-
one I knew," she mumbled, but he heard her.

The second the words were out of her mouth,
he watched in fascination the way his chest rose
and fell, as if he'd sustained a shock. "But that's
impossible."

She blinked, totally confused. "Why?"

"Only when a new male member of the royal
household is born is one minted. He wears it for
life and is buried with it."

The king's love for her grandmother must have
been beyond comprehension. "Did anyone see if
King Malik was buried with his?"

Rafi went so quiet, she knew he didn't have an
answer for that question. It was probably the only
time in his life he'd been thrown by a mystery he
couldn't solve.

Dark lines etched his arresting features.
'Tell me the name of the person he gave it to.
According to you, they're dead. You don't have to

worry since you've already broken your promise to them."

Tears pricked her eyelids. "Because you tricked me—"

"Not tricked. I only held off showing you the medallion until I could see that nothing else would work. It's my job to protect the royal family. I had to be certain you weren't working for a hostile entity sent to spy on the king or the acting sheikh."

"You mean Prince Rashad."

"That's right. You and I are both on the same side, Lauren."

Put that way, she realized they were, but she couldn't forgive him for what he'd put her through. She bit her lip. "H-he gave it to my grandmother," she said in a tremulous voice.

More silence. "When?" he eventually demanded.

"I'm sure if you went back far enough in the official documents of the kingdom, you would see that she traveled here alone, unmarried, when she was twenty years old.

"Someone told her about the Al-Shafeeq Oasis that blossomed like a rose in the desert. Being an adventurous person, she decided she wanted to see it."

Rafi stood there still as a statue. "She *met* Sheikh Malik?"

Lauren nodded. "He was twenty-six at the time. He saw her walking in the palace garden. She had hair my color, but she wore it down her back to her waist. He was so drawn to her, he had her brought to him. One thing led to another. At one point he took her to see the Garden of the Moon."

A strange sound came out of Rafi.

"It was there he told her he would love her until the day he died. But he couldn't marry her because he was betrothed to another princess."

Her voice shook as she told Rafi the rest. "H-he said she would have to leave the Oasis and they would never be able to see each other again. The only thing he could give her was the medallion.

He put it around her neck and told her that every time she looked at it, he would sense it and know she was remembering their time beneath the moon when she'd made him feel immortal."

Rafi rubbed the back of his neck. A white ring encircled his lips.

"When my grandmother knew she was dying she took the medallion off her own neck and gave it to me. She said that next to me, it was her most priceless possession. After she passed away, I had this longing to come to the oasis and see where it had all happened."

She undid the chain. "Thank you for returning this to me, but it isn't mine to keep. It belongs to the royal family. I would think King Umar would like to have something that belonged to his father. Princess Farah said that King Malik was known as the great sheikh for making the kingdom stronger.

"The more I think about it, the more I want him to have it in payment of his generosity and kindness to me while I've been recuperating at he palace." She went over to the desk and left it on top. "Now am I free to go?"

His eyes were dark slits as he looked at her. "No."

She struggled for breath. "Do you want me to stay, Rafi? If you do, tell me—"

He gave her a look so tormented, she was shaken by it. Without saying a word, he walked behind his desk and opened the drawer. She saw him take out a ring and put it on. Then he moved toward her and extended his hand, palm down.

When she saw the same medallion in the form of a ring, she got that curious din in her ears again, as she'd felt when the sandstorm had hit without warning. The same presentiment came to her now that she was about to go through another life-changing experience and nothing would ever be the same again.

One by one, every moment with him, every nuance, every warning, every word and gesture fell into place as pure revelation flowed through her. Her eyes searched his and she saw the truth written in them. She remembered him telling her that the kind of marriage she imagined wasn't written in his stars…

"*You're* Prince Rashad," she whispered.

No-o-o. Oh no—

She felt his hands cup her face and lift it. The eyes staring down at her blazed with fire. In panic, she tried to pull away from him, but he held her fast. "Don't be frightened of me, Lauren. You know I could never hurt you. Now that everything's out in the open and there are no secrets between us, all I want to do is love you."

"No—" She jerked away from him and staggered back. "We can't!—"

How could she have been so blind? He was the acting sheikh. Of course. Hadn't he talked and walked like a prince?

His hands slid to her shoulders, kneading them restlessly. "I need you and I know you need me. I have an apartment through that door. We'll start all over again and be alone for as long as we want. We'll do what we've been wanting to do from the very beginning. You're all I desire," he declared passionately, running his hands up and down her arms.

"You're all I want, too," she answered honestly. "You have no idea of the depth of my feelings, but we can't be together because—because it would be wrong!"

"Wrong?" He laughed almost angrily. "How can you say that when we know what we feel for each other is so right no power has been able to stop it?"

She agreed. There'd been something that had come over her before she'd even fully awakened after the sandstorm, bonding her to him. But she possessed a secret he didn't know anything about yet. Lauren could keep it to herself, but could she live with the guilt of it over a lifetime?

She already knew the answer to that question. No matter how much she wanted to belong to Rafi, she realized the knowledge would eventually destroy them both. She had to tell him the truth.

"Don't look at me like that, Lauren," he implored, misunderstanding the pain in her eyes.

"I'll go to my father tonight. When I explain to him about us, he'll call off the plans for my wedding. I couldn't go through with it now." He started kissing her face, every part of it, thrilling her so completely her body throbbed with need.

"Farah said it would take place at the end of the year."

He smothered a moan before clasping her hands and kissing her fingertips. "The timeline has changed to a month away. I have to go to him before another day passes."

Jealousy drove a shaft through Lauren. "Who is she?"

"It doesn't matter."

"Of course it matters. Already she's planning to be your wife. You can't undo what's been done."

"You think not?" he came back in a voice of command. "Princess Azzah will rejoice when she learns it's been called off."

No, she won't, Lauren lamented. Farah didn't

have to tell Lauren that her brother was desired by other women. There was no other man like him. "She's already anticipating her marriage to you."

His eyes, so black and alive, searched hers. "Why are you fighting me on this?"

"Because I'm not going to be the woman responsible for causing a breach with your father. When you and I were together the other night, I thought you were the king's chief of security. I thought you were emotionally free.

"When you told me you were a pot who still hadn't found its cover, I interpreted that to mean you were a bachelor who enjoyed the life you were living. But now that I know your identity, everything's changed.

"Farah has told me things. She says your father isn't well. One day you'll be taking his place. You have no choice but to carry on certain traditions for which your life has always been destined."

Lines marred his handsome features. "Your argument rings hollow. You're holding back

another secret from me. What else did Farah
tell you?"

"Nothing."

"That's not true. Why won't you look at me?"

"Rafi—I need to leave."

"You're not going anywhere." He grasped her
arms. "I want to know what my sister said to
you."

"It was just a passing comment, but it appears
to have come true." In fact Lauren was haunted
by it now.

She heard him expel an angry breath. "Is your
silence intended to be punishment for me because
of the way I dealt with you?"

"No—" she cried, hearing the anguish in his
voice. She lifted imploring eyes to him. "While
we were all at the pool the other day, she made
the passing comment you had been too favored.
She said your mother feared that because you'd
been given every gift there'd be a price to pay.

"I asked her what she thought her mother meant.
She said that heaven was jealous of you. One day

when something came along you wanted more than anything on earth, it wouldn't be granted."

Rafi bit out an epithet. She didn't have to know Arabic to understand the emotion behind it. "I love Farah, but she's a very dramatic, impressionable person who overstates things at times without realizing it."

"Nevertheless, she was right about this, wasn't she? You and I want something that can't be. I'm going to have to do what my grandmother did. Somehow she found the strength to leave King Malik and never come back. Now it's my turn to do the right thing."

"No," Rafi declared. "That's *not* the right thing for either of us. My nation has come out of the Dark Ages, Lauren. I've been doing everything possible to modernize our way of life and keep up with the new advances, particularly in technology.

"Change has been inevitable and will continue to happen. The point is, I'm not a product of another era. I was born into this one. Some tradi-

tions from the past are good and important. Ye
I have a different view of many things to make
life better for our people.

"Certainly I haven't grown up being in favor o
archaic marriage traditions, but until I met you, I
was willing to go along with my father's expectations. Now everything has changed. I refuse to
be like my grandfather who was so strong in his
own beliefs, he gave up the great love of his life
and sent your grandmother away. That decision
left them no joy."

When Rafi would have kissed her mouth,
Lauren hid her face from him. "Then I'll have
to be strong for both of us."

"Why?" he cried.

"Because King Malik was *my* grandfather, too."
Silence shattered everything.

As the revelation computed, his arms tightened
around her. "Say that again?" he whispered into
her hair.

With tears in her voice she said, "We both have
the same grandfather. My grandmother went

ome not realizing she was pregnant with my
mother. *Their* daughter."

His hands tightened in her curls before sliding
o her upper arms. He eased her far enough away
o look into her eyes. "But that's impossible."

"No. It was very possible, Rafi. They were
overs for a fortnight…i-in the garden suite."

Rafi's skin took on an ashen color.

"Though she never admitted it to me, I'm posi-
ive she wanted his child when she realized she
couldn't have him."

Unspeakable pain turned his features to a fac-
simile of his former self. "I don't believe you."

"A DNA test would provide definitive proof,
but I have something else that will convince you."

His eyes impaled her. "What proof?" In them
she saw grief so profound, she had to look away.

"It's even stronger evidence than the medal-
ion. I'll show you. In my wallet there are some
pictures of my mother."

She watched the struggle he was having to
swallow. "Let me see them."

Lauren moved out of his arms and reached fo her purse. Inside her wallet she kept a packet o pictures. She pulled out the three she'd put in o her parents. The first colored photo she handed him showed a full-length picture of Lana holding Lauren outside on the deck of her grandmother' apartment. At five months Lauren's golden hai had come in curly and gleamed in the sun.

Rafi took the photo in his fingers and looked at it, then at Lauren. "But this is a picture o Samira!"

"It's an amazing likeness of her. When I me your sister, I could see my mother in her. But i you'll look closely, you'll notice Lake Geneva is in the background and she's holding a *blonde* baby. That's me at five months."

"No," he moaned the word.

Gaunt with shock, he looked at the other two pictures she handed him. Both of them showed her blond father holding Lauren, with his arm around her mother.

A lifetime seemed to pass before a haunting

groan came out of him filled with soul-deep anguish. He caught her to him. They clung with a desperation that racked them both.

"Tell me this is a nightmare and we're going to wake up," he begged.

"I wish I could," she whispered, her agony beyond tears, "but you had to hear the truth. Celia named my mother Lana, an Arabic name. Our grandfather never knew. Neither did my mother. Celia told her that the man who was her father was just a man she'd met. Ships passing in the night.

"She claimed she never knew what happened to him, but it wasn't important because she and Lana had each other. That was all they needed."

A pulse throbbed at the corner of his mouth. "How could she have kept that news from my grandfather?"

She studied him through glazed eyes. "You of all people should know the answer to that question. His betrothal had taken place years before.

He sent Celia away so there'd be no scandal. She loved him too much to cause him any distress.

"My mother had to accept the explanation and let it go. A few minutes ago when I realized who you were, don't you think I wanted to die? Now I've got to let you go the same way."

When she eventually found the strength to ease away so she could look at him, she didn't recognize the man; he seemed to have aged ten years.

"Lauren—"

She forced herself to smile through the tears. "You have a phrase for everything. 'It is what it is.' That's what we have to say now."

"But it *isn't* what it is—" he fired back in pain. "I won't allow it to be." He shook her gently. "No one knows about this but you and me. We'll forget everything because I'm not losing you!" He crushed her mouth beneath his.

For a time she responded, losing track of time and place because she couldn't help herself. But then the reality of what they were doing took hold. Much as she wanted to kiss and be kissed

nto oblivion by him, the truth was between them
and she couldn't keep this up. It was no use.

As soon as he allowed her breath she said, "I
could wish you'd told me who you were that first
day. Then I would have closed my heart off to
you, or broken down and told you we had the
same grandfather. You always talk about fate. I'm
afraid this time it had something else in mind for
us.

"If only you could undo our history, Rafi, you
truly would be a god, but you're still mortal and
that means I have to go. Every minute I stay here,
it's making it that much harder to leave."

"I won't let you." He tightened his arms around
her, kissing her with refined savagery.

"We have no choice," she half sobbed the words.
"Don't you see?" She caught his face between her
hands. "We have two strikes against us. Even if
we weren't related, I can't remain here another
second and jeopardize the life you were born to
no matter what you say. You'll be king one day.
Princess Azzah will be your queen. It's written!"

Finding her inner strength, she escaped his arms and flew out of his office. Outside the building, Nazir ran after her, but she didn't stop until she reached the helicopter, out of breath. He helped her inside with a concerned look on his face.

"Tell the pilot to take me to El-Joktor immedi-ately. The prince has set me free. Please do this for me, Nazir. Please," she begged with all the strength of her soul.

"Yes, mademoiselle."

Since Lauren had fled from his arms like a sand devil spinning away with the speed of light, Rashad had sealed himself in his Raz apartment. Now that it was evening, the helicopter had come back for him.

During the short flight back to Al-Shafeeq Nazir reported that everything had gone smoothly at El-Joktor. He had walked Lauren on to the jet without problem. Since then, he had had word hat her flight had landed in Geneva. Was there anything else he could do for Rashad?

With nothing more to be done, Rashad assured him there'd be a big bonus in his paycheck for services rendered. After thanking the others, he went inside the palace and headed straight for his parents' suite. When he walked in, Farah came flying across the sitting room and threw her arms around his waist.

"I'm so sorry for speaking to you the way I did last night. Please forgive me, Rashad."

"There's nothing to forgive because I know love motivated you." He kissed her forehead. "I deserved it and a host of other things you didn't say."

"This morning I came to say goodbye to Lauren, but she'd already gone."

Rashad closed his eyes tightly. "She's in Geneva as we speak."

"You can pretend all you want, but I know you love her."

He studied his sister who'd always been there

for him. "I won't lie to you about that, but she'
gone now, so there's nothing more to be said.'
Their grandfather's blood flowed in Lauren'
veins, too. One couldn't jump high enough to
get over that camel's hump.

She touched his face. "You look ill."

"It will pass."

"No it won't!" she stamped her foot in a rare
show of temper. "Go in to the bedroom and tel
our father you can't go through with your mar
riage next month."

That checked him. "How did you know abou
the change of date?"

"Father's been looking for you all day and coul
not find you. No one knew where you were, no
even Nazir. Your phone has been turned off. He
got so upset he called the entire family and tol
everyone to look for you.

"I knew you were with Lauren, but I didn't say
anything to give you away. When I asked him
why he was so upset, he let it slip that you have to

let Sheikh Majid know of your agreement about the new date for the wedding by tomorrow night."

"I'll go in to father now. Is mother with him?"

"No. She's still talking to the chef about the meal preparations for our birthday party in a few days. You know how she is." Farah's eyes filled with liquid. "She wants everything perfect for us, for you. So do I, but I know you're never going to know joy. You can't go through with this wedding, Rashad. It won't be fair to you or to Princess Azzah."

Rashad ran a hand over his face in despair. As he'd found out this morning, life wasn't fair. "Bless you for being you, Farah." He kissed her once more, then strode quickly to the bedroom where his father sat on the side of the bed with his bad foot propped on an ottoman piled with cushions.

His father simply stared at him. He didn't need to speak. Rashad already knew every word he would say if he chose to express himself.

"Farah met me in the sitting room. Forgive me for giving you a scare, father. I—"

"You need explain nothing. I have my own eyes and ears around the palace. If I didn't, I wouldn't have lived this long. The American. Is she gone?"

"Yes."

His father's dark eyes pierced through to Rashad's soul. "For good?"

A boulder lodged in his throat. "Yes."

"Good. Did you send her away with your baby?"

Rashad threw his head back in torment. "No. There's no possibility."

"That's even better. The wound that bleeds inwardly is the most dangerous. Tell me what's going on that has you writhing body and soul."

Rashad's pacing came to a halt. "When we buried grandfather four months ago, was he wearing his medallion?"

The change of subject caught his father off guard. "Who told you he wasn't?" he snapped uncharacteristically.

Pain shot through Rashad. Lauren's truth *was* the truth. He was crucified all over again with that knowledge.

"No one," he whispered.

"Since you know he wasn't wearing it, why did you ask me?"

Rashad shook his head. "It doesn't matter. I just wanted you to know it's been found." He reached in his pocket and drew out the medallion and chain. After staring at it for a minute, he put it in his father's hand.

Dumbfounded, his father eyed Rashad strangely. "How did *you* come by it?"

Rashad drew up a chair next to him. "The American woman was wearing it around her neck when I flew her to the palace more dead than alive."

His father's eyes filled with wonder. "Go on."

"Yes. Go on," his mother said. She'd come in the bedroom without Rashad being aware of it. She looked like an older version of Basmah, tall and lovely. She sat down on the bed next to his father.

For the next little while Rashad told them everything from the beginning, leaving nothing out. When he'd finished, his father said, "And throughout all this business, you fell in love."

"Yes." Rashad jumped up from the chair unable to contain his emotions. "But she has Grandfather's blood in her just as I do." Nothing could have shocked him more in his life. No news could have devastated him more.

His father nodded. "Now I understand why you feel you can never see her again."

Rashad stared at his parents for a long time. " realize I'm a great disappointment to the two of you, but what I felt for her went beyond honor or duty the moment I carried her from the sand to the helicopter. It felt as though she'd been delivered to me. For me…

"Before I found out we had a grandfather in common, I planned to come to you and tell you couldn't go through with the marriage to Princess

Azzah because I intended to marry Lauren. When I took her to the Garden of the Moon, I realized I couldn't live without her."

His mother eyed him with tenderness. "That doesn't surprise me. You've always been led by what you believed in your heart, Rashad. I've been listening to everything you've said." She looked at his father. "I think it's time we told him, Umar. Don't you? I know we agreed not to as long as it wasn't necessary, but now I know that it is."

"Tell me what?" He couldn't imagine.

"If you want to know the answer, you need to be patient enough to sit down and listen to a story," his father chastised him.

His mother smiled. "It's a story you'll like."

That's what she'd always said when he was a boy too restless to hear all the words between the beginning and the end.

"Forgive me, Mother, but I'm not eight years old anymore."

"No," she murmured. "That's why you have to listen to your father."

His father cleared his throat. "It begins on the night I was camped on the desert with our patrol because there'd been a raid on one of our village and we were keeping a watch out for more. decided to scout around. My right hand, Saud rode with me."

Yes. He knew. There was no man Umar had loved more than his childhood friend, Saud, but Rashad had heard the story many times of how Saud had protected his father from death before meeting his own, and he couldn't imagine what this was leading up to.

"The assassins had stormed through Saud's village first and killed many of the women and children, Saud's wife included."

Yes, he knew that, too. His father had ridden to that village and had found her lying in a pool of blood.

"What you don't know was that she'd delivered a baby that night who lay under her."

That did surprise, Rashad. His eyes swerved to his father's.

"He was still alive."

CHAPTER EIGHT

ON the morning following her flight from Al-Shafeeq, Lauren drove to the cemetery and put white daisies on all three of the family graves. She lingered over her grandmother's.

"I took the trip you took, Grandmother, and guess what? I, too, fell in love with a great Prince of the desert, but our love wasn't meant to be. Instead of bringing home his baby beneath my heart, I have two cigar boxes, one with his father's image on the top, the other of your beloved Malik. I don't even have a photograph of Rafi." Tears dropped onto the marker.

"Like you, I can't go back to get one. All I could do was leave the medallion. It's in the hands of the man I love. Help me find a way to survive, Grandmother. *Please.*"

Unwilling for people to see her in this condition, Lauren hurriedly left the cemetery and
drove back to the apartment. She knew she had
to keep busy or go insane and decided she would
start some major housecleaning. One day soon
she'd phone her friends, but not right now.

After parking her car on the street behind two
limos, she got out, then came to a complete stand-
still. At least ten men wearing native robes and
headscarves blocked the main entrance. Her heart
jumped at the sight of them.

"Mademoiselle Viret?"

"Nazir—" she cried, shocked at the sound of
the familiar voice.

He walked over to her. "Bonjour, mademoiselle." He smiled. "Please forgive the intrusion.
If you would be so good as to come with us, we'll
escort you to the plane King Umar has sent for
you." The group had surrounded her, leaving her
with little room to maneuver.

Her legs felt like water. "Don't you mean Prince

Rashad?" Why would he do this now? It was a cruelty she wouldn't have expected of him. There could be nothing between them.

"No, mademoiselle. The king wishes you to return immediately. He would have come, but he can't travel in his condition. He asks if you will be kind enough to spend a few days at Al-Shafeeq with him and his family. He would like to meet Princess Lauren, the American grand-daughter of King Malik."

Princess—

This meant Rashad had told his father everything. Lauren couldn't stop her body from trembling. "Much as I would love to meet him I can't." She needed to root Rafi out of her heart. Of course that would never be possible, but to return to Al-Shafeeq...

"Prince Rashad predicted you would say that. He asked me to tell you that he will be away from the palace while you're there."

Her pain grew worse.

"Since he won't be present, he says there's no

eason for you not to come. It will make his father and mother and his sisters very happy, *unless* you can't forgive him for a deception he felt compelled to carry out at the time for the safety of his family."

She rubbed her temples where she felt a headache coming on from all her crying.

"He at least asks you to forgive him as you would one who believes that the ways of his tribe are the laws of nature."

Oh, Rafi. Another one of his unique sayings that made her want to laugh and cry at the same time. This one wound its way into her heart with the rest of them.

She bit her lip. "Are you saying the king wants me to come now?"

"Yes. He hoped it would be a good time since you haven't yet settled back in to your home here."

Rafi might not be at the Oasis right now, but he knew her whereabouts and had eyes in the back of his head. "I would have to pack."

"The prince says that unlike other tourists you are a master at packing lightly. He is very impressed."

Oh Rafi...

"The King urges you to come. He says to remind you he's not well. He may not be your father, but you share the same blood and he already loves you as his half-daughter. He's aware your own father died before you could get to know him. Will you please accept him as your second father and allow him to spoil you a little bit?"

Her eyes smarted. Sheer blackmail.

Like father like son.

Lauren found King Umar to be much like any father and grandfather, surrounded by his family and loving it. The real miracle was that Lauren was a legitimate part of that family. He and his wife accepted her as if she were their long-lost daughter.

For three days they'd gathered at meal times

n the king's sitting room to hear the story of her grandmother's great love affair with King Malik.

Naturally the conversation turned to Lauren and the things she'd done with her life. The older children bombarded her with questions about the places she'd traveled, the sights she'd seen when Richard Bancroft had been alive to take her on some of his expeditions.

On the third afternoon, Farah asked Lauren to go on a horseback ride with her around the perimeter of the Oasis. Knowing she'd ridden Zia before, Abdul had the mare saddled and ready for her. The horse made a nickering sound and nudged Lauren in greeting. When she mounted her, the memories were so overwhelming, it was almost debilitating for her.

"The family loves you, Lauren." She and Farah rode side by side. Their bodyguards went along at a discreet distance.

"I love all of you."

"Before you leave, there's something you should know."

Lauren couldn't do this anymore. "Farah—if this is about your brother, I'd rather nothing was said."

"But you need to know he talked to my father on the day you flew to Geneva. Whatever was said, his wedding to the princess was called off permanently."

A moan escaped her lips. "What a sad day for everyone."

"Not for Rashad. He couldn't marry a woman he didn't love."

Lauren gripped the reins so tightly, it cut off the circulation in her hands. "Does this mean your father will allow him to choose the woman he wishes to marry?"

"I don't know. But since he didn't force him to marry Princess Azzah, I have to hope he won't command him to marry someone else who will mean nothing to him."

At the thought of Rashad choosing a woman he could eventually love, physical pain attacked

Lauren. "I'm sorry, Farah, but I can't talk about this. I can't."

"I'm sorry if I have distressed you. Come. We'll go back. The family is planning a special farewell dinner for you."

"Everyone has done more than enough for me."

"You still don't understand, do you? My father has asked you to stay here and live with us."

"I know, and I'm very touched, but I couldn't. My life is in Switzerland."

"Life is where your heart is," Farah corrected her.

Lauren had no answer for that. They rode back to the palace in silence.

After a long swim, the two of them parted company so they could get ready for dinner. Once back in the garden suite, Lauren showered and put on a filmy plum-colored sundress with spaghetti straps.

Because of King Umar's poor health, they ate all their meals in his sitting room, this farewell dinner being no exception. Seventeen family members gathered round.

Lauren and her grandmother had been a two some before Richard had come along to make i three. To belong to such a big family now coulc have been a real joy except for one thing. One person…

Rafi's absence was the camel in the room n one talked about. Lauren missed him so acutely she wasn't able to concentrate on the conversa tions going on around her. Tomorrow couldn' come soon enough to end this pain. The king insisted on flying her back to Geneva in his pri vate jet if she wished to go.

After coffee, he clapped his hands to get every one's attention. "One of my duties as king is t secure husbands for my daughters, which I hav done. Since my father, King Malik, can't be her tonight to secure a husband for his granddaugh ter, Princess Lauren, the great honor has faller to me."

Lauren had been eating a sugar-coated almond and almost choked on it.

"As I have the power to act in his stead, I've chosen a man of our tribe who is in every way worthy to be your husband. In a few minutes you will meet him and tomorrow formal negotiations will be made for your marriage."

Her eyes widened. Surely the king didn't mean it, yet when she looked around, everyone was staring at her with a pleased expression—except Farah.

The princess got to her feet. "You can't do this, Father. She's not used to our traditions."

Lauren loved Farah for defending her. What the king had just said might have made sense to him, but it was impossible!

He nodded his graying head. "Nevertheless, it is not your place to counsel me, Farah," he spoke kindly. "Please sit down. Lauren has no one to protect her. We are her family now and must do what is best for her."

"But—"

"No buts. You've told me on more than one occasion that you have been very happy with my choice of husband for you. Therefore, you trust my judgment, don't you?"

"Yes, but—"

"Silence, my daughter."

He clapped his hands. Lauren heard the doors to the suite open. She jerked around in absolute panic and saw Rafi in the entry wearing a cream silk robe. Her heart turned into a battering ram as he walked into the room and sat down next to his father.

Nazir had assured her Rafi would stay away from the palace during her visit, yet here he was with that tall powerful body, looking more princely than any prince. The king must have insisted his son come to watch, but she couldn't do this, and she jumped to her feet.

She felt Rafi's piercing gaze on her, but she kept her eyes focused on King Umar. "Princess Farah was right, Your Highness. Though the last thing I would ever want to do is offend you,

can't go through with this because I don't wish
to be married."

"You would say that to me, knowing I want
to take care of a great wrong done to one of my
family?"

"Forgive me, Your Highness, but it would be a
much greater wrong if I were forced to marry a
man I didn't love no matter how much I appreciate your wanting to take care of me."

"You prefer to live a solitary life and die of old
age without knowing love or children?"

"Millions of women in the world do it," she
stood her ground.

"Not *our* women," he came back.

"Putting aside my feelings for a minute, what
about the man you would force to marry me? He
would be a stranger to me."

"You will learn to adapt to each other's differ-
ences. A lifetime study to make the other person
happy is one of the most exciting aspects of marriage. Let me give you an example. When my

wife, Tahirah, and I started out, we were blessed with three baby girls.

"But during the pregnancy with Farah—which had taken a long time to happen—there were problems. Dr. Tamam said that once the baby was delivered, my wife would never be able to have another baby.

"We realized it wasn't written in the stars, but deep inside I knew my wife suffered because she could never give me a son. Deep inside *I* suffered because I knew she was suffering and I couldn't take her condition away.

"The night Farah was born, I was away fighting. It was at that same time my best friend Saud died saving my life. That night I learned his wife Fadwa, had been killed in a village raid. When I found her body, I discovered she'd just delivered a baby boy who was still alive.

"I took him home to my wife, only to discover our little Farah lying in her arms. When I showed her Saud's son, she loved him on sight and asked f we couldn't keep him and raise him as our own. That was the wish of my heart, too, so the wo babies became our twins. Only Dr. Tamam knew our secret."

All around Lauren she heard gasps, but none were greater than her own.

"Nothing could have made us happier. A life for a life. Though Saud's and his wife's deaths came at the appointed hour, their child's did not. Together, Tahirah and I vowed to raise him as if he'd been born from our bodies.

"I called him Rashad in honor of his birth father who was a man of flawless integrity. My wife called him Rayhan, the favoured one. His best friend called him Rafi, the exalted one."

Rafi...

"He's headstrong and modern-thinking. Indeed, he's so much like Saud, who always had vision, t has been as if I had my friend back in the form of his perfect son."

His wife nodded. "Rashad has been so perfect, there's been no princess to measure up to him.

We feared we'd never find one good enough for him which is why we hadn't forced a marriage before now. But with his thirty-fifth birthday approaching, we picked Princess Azzah in desperation. She had some of the qualities we knew Rashad would admire."

King Umar nodded. "Then fate worked its will once more, and my father's granddaughter suddenly appeared out of the desert, more royal than any princess we could have found for our son.

"You have Shafeeq blood flowing through your veins, Lauren." He smiled at her. "We know Rashad very well and recommend him highly. He will make you a fine husband. Your marriage will secure the sheikhdom for Rashad after I'm gone."

Lauren's gaze fused with Rafi's as he started across the room toward her, but she was feeling light-headed. The last thing she remembered hearing was Farah's squeal of happiness before everything began to spin.

When she regained consciousness, her eyelids

fluttered open and she became aware Rafi had brought her to the garden suite. She was lying on her bed.

"Rafi?"

He poured a glass of water for her. "Drink this first," he said emotionally, cradling the back of her head to help her.

Lauren stared at his beloved face while she drank. It was déjà vu for the third or fourth time. She'd lost track.

When he put the glass on the bedside table, she raised up on one elbow. His concerned black eyes made a swift inventory of her features. "Your color's coming back."

"What happened?"

"You fainted when my father said I would make you a good husband. I need to know if you did that because something has changed and you don't want to be my wife. He insisted on handling everything his way. I know it made him happier than he's been in years, but the truth is,

I came close to having a heart attack when you slumped in my arms."

"You caught me?" she cried out in wonder.

"I watched your face start to turn white and acted before you slid to the floor. Don't ever do that to me again, darling. I couldn't take it."

"I've never fainted in my life." She looped her arms around his neck and pulled him down. He stretched out on the bed beside her. "I think i might have been because I had been granted the wish of my heart and my body couldn't take in that much joy all at once. A miracle has happened to us," she cried. *"Oh, Rafi—"*

She started kissing him all over his face, his hair, his neck. "Don't move. Don't leave me I'm going to need till morning to believe this i really happening to us. I love my grandmother for giving me the medallion. I'm crazy about your parents for loving you enough to hold off on finding you a wife until I blew into your life I love and adore you so terribly, it hurts."

"Even when I was so cruel to you on our camp-out?" he whispered against her lips.

"I knew there had to be a reason. The more I saw of you, the more I wanted to be with you. I lived for the moments you walked in this suite. Every time I saw you, I couldn't wait to find out what little tortures you had in store for me. At the Garden of the Moon I was shameless with desire for you."

"Do you think a woman with less fire or passion could ever have held me?" he cried huskily. "Those were gifts I never planned on in this life. Then, when I thought they were miraculously within reach, it was all snatched away by your confession about our grandfather. My heart came close to dying."

"So did mine."

He kissed her deeply, then fastened the chain with the medallion around her neck. "I love you, Lauren. Marry me."

She touched it, feeling the warmth of his fingers against the metal. "I already feel married to you. Does that shock you?"

"No, *kalida*. It thrills and humbles me."

"Kalida?"

"My love, my darling." He sealed the endearment with another kiss that swept her away.

When she could breathe again she said, "I've been thinking about what to do with all my money, my inheritance. I want it to go into a fund for some of your big plans for the kingdom. My grandmother will be entirely approving. Anything you want, but I'll hold a little of it back to hire more bodyguards to protect you. I'm determined to stave off your appointed time until we're old and can die together."

"Your wish is my command."

When Lauren's cell phone rang, she felt too nauseous to turn on her other side and reach for it. But she made the effort anyway because it might be her husband. He'd wanted to make love this morning before leaving for Raz early, but she'd pretended to be asleep so he wouldn't know how sick she felt.

One look at the caller ID and she realized it was Farah calling. Making another superhuman effort, she clicked on and said hello to her sister-in-law.

"Good morning, Lauren. How would you like to go riding with me this morning?"

"Much as I'd love to, I'm feeling a little under the weather. Perhaps tomorrow morning. Please don't tell anyone else. I'm hoping it will pass because I don't want Rafi worrying about me. He has enough on his mind right now winding up the completion of the new smelter."

"Do you feel too awful for a visitor?"

Farah was excited about something. After four months of living at the palace, Lauren was adept at reading her moods. "No. Just walk in. I barely woke up and am still in bed."

"I'll be right there."

No sooner had Lauren hung up, than she had to dash to the bathroom where she was promptly sick. After rinsing out her mouth and brushing her teeth, she felt a little better, but she'd clearly caught some kind of bug. Yesterday morning she'd felt it coming on. Oddly enough tea and a roll suddenly sounded good to her.

She rang the housekeeper and asked that a tray be sent. Enough for two. Then she got back in Rafi's bed. They'd been living in his suite. As soon as he could take a few days off, they were going to fly to Switzerland. She planned to put the apartment up for sale and have all her things shipped to Al-Shafeeq. What they couldn't use she would put in storage. Rafi wanted her to be completely happy.

While her thoughts were on her fantastic husband, Farah arrived at the same time as the maid and brought the breakfast tray into the bedroom. She put it on the coffee table and flashed Lauren a speculative glance.

"I thought you didn't feel well."

"Right after I got off the phone with you, I was sick in the bathroom. Now I'm hungry."

"How long has this been going on?"

Lauren blinked. "I started feeling queasy yesterday morning."

Farah's dark eyes lit up with excitement. "Both my pregnancies started off exactly like that. I bet you're carrying Rashad's baby."

Lauren slid off the bed and hurried over to hug Farah. "If I thought that were true, I'd fly to Raz and tell him."

"Then get dressed and go to the clinic. Dr Tamam will verify one way or the other. If you're not pregnant, then Rashad will want to know why you're ill because he watches every move you make. Honestly, Lauren, he's so in love with you it's sickening…in the most wonderful way of course."

"I feel the same way about him." She bit into a roll and followed it with several swallows of sweet tea.

Farah smiled. "The whole palace knew the day after you arrived here the first time."

A blush crept up Lauren's neck and cheeks "I'm sure they do." She finished off her roll "Before I get dressed and take your advice, tel me what you wanted to talk to me about."

"Well, Abdul and I have made a decision. Sinc Father and Mother told us Rashad wasn't thei blood child, it has convinced us to adopt a baby At first I was afraid to do it because I didn't thinl I could be a good mother. But when I see Rasha and Mother together, I know she loves him as i she'd given birth to him."

"Oh, Farah—" Lauren reached out and hugged her again, much harder this time. "That's the most wonderful news I ever heard. Now, come to the clinic with me and we'll see what the wise doctor has to say about me."

While Rashad was inspecting the smelter, he saw three helicopters from his father's fleet headed for Raz. Something had to be wrong, He whipped out his phone and called Nazir to find out what was going on.

"Nothing I've been informed about, Your Highness."

With his heart starting to thud, Rashad rang off and left the smelter for the area where the helicopters were about to land. Soon the doors opened and more guards poured out followed by a golden-haired woman. Lauren!

She jumped down and ran toward him.

He caught her in his arms and swung her around. Her fragrance, the feel of her body intoxicated him. "What are you doing here? You've never flown to Raz to see me before."

Her head fell back so she could look into his eyes. The light green of hers between those dark lashes dazzled him. "Forgive me for intruding, but something important has happened and I couldn't wait to tell you. I'll go inside your office until you can take a break."

"We'll go together. I decided not to eat lunch so I could get home faster to you this afternoon."

With their arms wrapped around each other's waists, they entered the building and hurried toward his office suite. Once inside, he closed the door and locked it.

"It's so hot! You need some water first." She would have gone over to his mini fridge to get him a bottle, but he pulled her back.

"First I need *this!*" His dark head descended and his mouth covered hers, devouring her with shocking hunger, as if they'd never kissed before. "I missed you this morning," he confessed on a ragged breath.

She knew what he meant. "I wanted you more than anything, too, but I didn't feel well. I've just been consulting with Dr. Tamam, actually. It's why I'm here."

In the next instant he took a shuddering breath and his hands tightened around her upper arms. She saw that white ring encircle his seductive mouth; she had come to recognize it as fear. "I've been too happy," his voice throbbed. "Tell me what's wrong with you." She actually saw tears in his eyes.

Lauren stood on tiptoe to kiss his lips, but they refused to cooperate until she gave him his answer. "I'm two months pregnant. We're either going to have a little Saud or a little Fadwa. Your birth parents made the most gorgeous son who ever lived. With you as the father of our child, we'll have to keep him or her scarfed for protection."

An explosion of joy lit up the deep recesses of Rafi's eyes. He picked Lauren up and carried her through to his apartment. Over the last four months he'd taken her to his bed more times than he wanted anyone to know about, but he'd never put her down so gently before. She was a miracle to him. He slid his hand over her stomach to feel her.

Her heart shone out of her eyes. "Rafi, it'll be a few months before we feel the little one kicking, but our baby's in there. The doctor has given me some medicine to help with my morning sickness. I hope that tomorrow morning I'll be able to wake you up first.

"I love mornings with you, Rafi. But then, love every second of the day and night with you I told Dr. Tamam I have a sickness because of you. Do you know what he said?"

"What?" he whispered, tracing her delectable mouth with his finger.

"That you were the luckiest of men to have a wife with such a sickness. He said he would pray that I'd go to my grave with it." She kissed his finger. "I told him not to bother. He'd do better to pray that I don't wear you out with my love. That's the reason I haven't come to Raz before now. I haven't wanted to distract you from your work."

He rolled her over carefully on top of him. " dare you to try."

"You mean now?"

"Now," he growled into her neck.

Lauren's breath caught. "Don't you have to go back to work?"

"No. I've got all the work I can handle right here."

"Hours and hours?" she asked, already out of breath.

"Maybe days."

"Darling."

* * * * *

Mills & Boon® Large Print

October 2011

PASSION AND THE PRINCE
Penny Jordan

FOR DUTY'S SAKE
Lucy Monroe

ALESSANDRO'S PRIZE
Helen Bianchin

MR AND MISCHIEF
Kate Hewitt

HER DESERT PRINCE
Rebecca Winters

THE BOSS'S SURPRISE SON
Teresa Carpenter

ORDINARY GIRL IN A TIARA
Jessica Hart

TEMPTED BY TROUBLE
Liz Fielding

Mills & Boon® Large Print
November 2011

THE MARRIAGE BETRAYAL
Lynne Graham

THE ICE PRINCE
Sandra Marton

DOUKAKIS'S APPRENTICE
Sarah Morgan

SURRENDER TO THE PAST
Carole Mortimer

HER OUTBACK COMMANDER
Margaret Way

A KISS TO SEAL THE DEAL
Nikki Logan

BABY ON THE RANCH
Susan Meier

GIRL IN A VINTAGE DRESS
Nicola Marsh